Advance Praise for
MY LOVER IS A FREEDOM FIGHTER

*"Peel away layers of media manipulation, racial and
religious bigotry, and complacency toward people far
off, and read a story. Abdullah and Fatina navigate the
labyrinth of marriage common to many, through circumstances beyond the experience of most. Despite the bitter
realities of occupied Gaza, Rana Shubair teaches us love."*
—KEVIN HADDUCK, poet, writing teacher and
college administrator, Carroll College, Montana

"Rana Shubair writes from the heart."
—DON JACQUES, retired professor of Latin and
ancient Greek, Carroll College, Montana

*"Like a flower growing through a crack in the
concrete pavement, love flourishes in Gaza amid
the suffering brought on by a brutal colonizer,
reminding us that the people of Gaza are humans
too, and entitled to live in freedom and dignity."*
—NORMA HASHIM, treasurer of Viva Palestina
Malaysia and editor of *The Prisoners' Diaries* and
Dreaming of Freedom: *Palestinian Child Prisoners Speak*

My Lover
Is a
Freedom
Fighter

Rana Shubair

Cover and interior design by David Provolo
Production by Domini Dragoone
Cover photo by Alaa Alashi

print ISBN: 978-0-578-49697-9
ebook ISBN: 978-0-578-49806-5

www.RanaShubair.com
SkyLimit Press

10 9 8 7 6 5 4 3 2 1

To those who sacrifice,
bearing the torch of freedom
and giving light to Palestine.

FOREWORD

Gaza—the place of a million plots and a thousand narratives; where fear is the norm and joy is loud, raucous, and unapologetic; where amputees are more commonplace than washing machines and spent tear-gas grenades are used as strawberry pots. In Gaza, bullet wounds are just accessories to survival—growing pains that every Palestinian child must either dodge, endure, or succumb to eventually—and long life is a momentous achievement. In Gaza—the killing field of Israel—beneath the devastating shadow of shells, smoke, and shrapnel, and indeed, despite Israel, maybe even in defiance of Israel, there's a Palestinian love story to cherish. Rana Shubair has written a tale of human resilience, where the tenderness of love survives untouched against all odds, just as "the stars," she writes, "keep shining" no matter what dark cruelty is played out beneath them.

Rana is no stranger to the deadly destruction of Israel's wars. A steadfast survivor of three major bombardments and a mourner at more funerals than most of her collective readers, Rana knows Gaza. She knows how it lives, hides, fights, survives, runs, tunnels, suffocates, breathes, and loves. But how does love, in all its simplicities and all its complexities, survive victorious in the face of such adversity? Read on to find out....

—Sarah Wilkinson

SARAH WILKINSON is an English activist who began her career as a graphic designer and illustrator—from window design to maps, magazines, cookbooks, children's fiction, educational textbooks, and supportive learning materials to over 13 years with an international newspaper, where she moved into journalism and editing. She has been a supporter of Palestine for more than 30 years and a vocal and proactive campaigner since the First Intifada.

Maps of Palestine

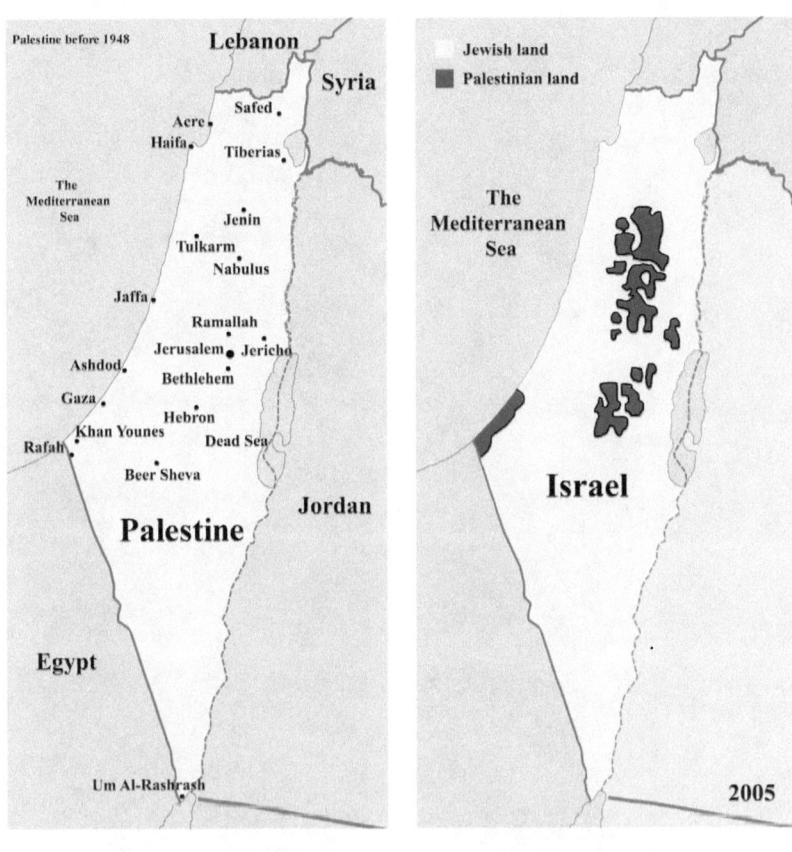

Palestine before 1948

Lebanon

Syria

Acre
Haifa
Safed
Tiberias

The Mediterranean Sea

Jenin
Tulkarm
Nabulus

Jaffa

Ramallah
Jerusalem Jericho
Ashdod
Bethlehem
Gaza
Hebron
Khan Younes
Rafah   Dead Sea

Beer Sheva

Palestine

Jordan

Egypt

Um Al-Rashrash

Jewish land
Palestinian land

The Mediterranean Sea

Israel

2005

PROLOGUE

On November 2nd, 1917, Britain decided, at the stroke of a pen, to give the Zionists a gift. The only problem was the gift they offered belonged to the Palestinian people. The British, who had no claim to Palestine, gave it away to the Zionists who had no right to it. It was included in the terms of the British Mandate of Palestine after World War I. The main goal of the British Mandate of Palestine was to create the conditions for the establishment of a Jewish "national home."

Jews had constituted less than 10 percent of the population at the time of the Mandate. The Balfour Declaration promised Jews a land where the natives made up more than 90 percent of the population. Upon the start of the mandate, the British began to facilitate the immigration of European Jews to Palestine. Between 1922 and 1935, the Jewish population rose from nine percent to nearly 27 percent of the total population. By 1947 the Jewish population increased to 33%.

This ominous pledge from Balfour is one of the main catalysts of the *Nakba*—the ethnic cleansing of Palestine in 1948—when Zionist militants, trained by the British, forcibly and violently expelled more than 750,000 Palestinians from their homeland. Those expelled and displaced from their homes fled to Gaza, the West Bank, Lebanon, Syria and Jordan. In Gaza Strip alone, 75% of the current population are refugees living in eight different camps across the Strip.

Gaza Strip was part of historic Palestine before the state of Israel was created in 1948. It was occupied by Israel in 1967 in the Six Day War. In 1987, and after 20 years of Israeli military occupation, the first Palestinian Uprising (Intifada) broke out. Palestinians began an intense resistance to the Israeli occupation. When the Intifada ended in 1993 with the signing of the Oslo Accords between the Palestinian Liberation Movement and Israel, approximately 1,392 Palestinians had been killed and more than 16,000 injured. The main terms of the Accords were that a peaceful political process was the only viable path to Palestinian statehood.

In the year 2000, a highly provocative move by Israeli politician Ariel Sharon was the act that triggered the second Intifada. Sharon's action violated the status quo of Jerusalem. Heavily guarded by Israeli soldiers, Sharon stormed into the Al-Aqsa mosque, the third most holy mosque in Islam. Fighting broke out, and seven Palestinians were killed. What became known as *Intifadat Al-Aqsa* began. Four days into the Intifada, twenty more Palestinians were killed, but the Palestinians fiercely resisted the occupation forces.

As things on the ground kept escalating, Palestinian factions turned to armed resistance while the Palestinian Authority took to peaceful negotiations, which led to nowhere. In 2005, Israel disengaged its troops from Gaza Strip. The number of Palestinians killed was 4,412 killed and 48, 322 were injured. As for Israeli losses, they totaled to 1,069.

Up to 2005, approximately 8,600 Israeli settlers lived in illegal settlements in the Gaza Strip. Gush Qatif was a block of 21 settlements in southern Gaza, where special roads were made for settlers' use only. Road 230 ran southwest along the Mediterranean Sea and Road 240 ran parallel to the sea, approximately one kilometer inland. These roads were built for the exclusive use of settlers. In August 2005, Ariel Sharon ordered disengagement from Gaza Strip, and all settlers were evacuated.

In 2006, the Palestinian Authority held parliamentary elections for the Palestinian Legislative Council. The two dominant, contesting parties were Hamas and Fatah, with other parties, like the Palestinian Popular Front, participating. The elections were internationally monitored and hailed as democratic by the world. But this victory was unexpected. Soon the new government, led by Hamas, was boycotted by the USA and European Union, and Israel imposed a blockade on the Gaza Strip that is still in effect to this day, in 2019.

The blockade means tight restrictions on freedom of movement for any purpose, including medical treatment. It also includes reducing fishing zones, firing at, capturing, and killing fishermen in open sea, further preventing entry of essential goods and medicines. It also cuts entry of fuel needed for operating the power plant. Sometimes citizens only get four hours of electricity daily. Half of the working-age population is unemployed, and the economic situation is dire. The building industry has grinded to a halt, thus costing the livelihoods of many thousands of workers.

To make the situation worse, Israeli occupation, at its will, chooses to launch attacks on Gaza Strip. In December of 2008, it launched a wide scale military aggression dubbed Operation Cast Lead, killing of about 1400 Palestinians, including 400 women and children, and wiping out entire families. Sixteen members of the Rayyan family were killed when an F-16 shelled their home. Houses, apartment buildings, factories and schools were bombed by Israeli war planes, leaving shocking destruction.

In 2012, the attack was repeated under the name *Pillar of Defense*. It started with the assassination of a chief of the Hamas military wing, Ahmed Al-Jabari, by shelling his car. The onslaught lasted for eight days, leaving around 167 Palestinians killed, including ten members of Al-Dalu family.

In 2014, Israel launched another attack, *Protective Edge,* killing over 2,000 people, including women and children, and wiping out entire families and neighborhoods. The official death toll was 2,145, including 578 children and 263 women. The attack lasted for 51 bloody days. All of these attacks were launched upon a defenseless population, who were also blockaded and suffering from a deprivation of basic human needs.

Palestinian resistance has been developing continuously. When all political efforts failed, the Gazans took matters into their own hands and shouldered the responsibility to protect the citizens from the vicious Israeli attacks. By doing this, they exercised the right to resist occupation as recognized and endorsed by international humanitarian laws and the additional Protocol I to the Geneva Conventions.

With further deterioration of the humanitarian situation in Gaza Strip and with no signs of alleviating the blockade, the Palestinians turned to peaceful demonstration in a call for the right to return to their stolen lands and for lifting the illegal blockade.

On March 30th of 2018, the Palestinians of Gaza decided to practice their right to peaceful assembly, near the fence which separates them from the homes and lands they lost in 1948. Up to the day this book was published, the number of protestors killed at the fence had reached 266 with an additional 25,477 injured. The protestors were met with Israeli snipers, stationed behind sand hills beyond the fence and firing high velocity rifles. Israeli Occupation Forces snipers have shot (often in the back) children, paramedics, and journalists. Top Israeli officials boast, "We know where every bullet went."

It is in this world of life under occupation, persever-ance and defiance that *My Lover Is A Freedom Fighter* takes place. The characters of my story are fictional, yet they represent the lives of resistance fighters here and how they opened their eyes to a world of occupation. They chose a role imposed upon them by the inhumane and brutal circumstance under which they live. The crushing stories of murder and displacement are passed on from one generation to another. Every generation takes part in the liberation process, in the hope that the children of the next generation may enjoy freedom and dignity. The collective punishment which the Israeli occupation imposes on the entire population of Gaza, supposedly in response to Hamas violence, has left no one safe.

This story follows Abdullah and Fatina, as they make their way through the intense crisis and the madness of life under occupation. Wherever they are, whatever they do, the reality which they live in is too stark to ignore or run away from. The scarce moments of peace they may enjoy could unexpectedly be inter-rupted by sudden attacks from above. They endure the loss of loved ones in the struggle. The deep pain inflicted upon them paralyzes them at times and they have to find a way to get back up. In this atmosphere, of love, loss and struggle, Fatina and Abdullah hold to each other and on to their beautiful dreams of love, peace and freedom.

PERSISTENCE

*Despite the death all around us, life has a strange
way of moving ahead. On one street, a martyr is
being carried away, while on the next street over,
there's a bachelor party taking place.*
—Fatina

In Fatina's neighborhood, as in the rest of the Gaza
Strip, bachelor parties were one of life's necessities.
Held on the street outside the groom's house, each
party lasted from sunset until midnight. Preparations
start early. First, a stage is erected and decorated with
colorful lights. Local singers perform, torturing the
neighborhood with their cacophony of voices. Despite
this, people still hire them to give a Gaza-style performance. Nonetheless, the guests immerse themselves in
the festive atmosphere.

Fatina watched from her living room window as a groom's friends carried him down the street and tossed him high in the air, chanting raucous remarks about his last night as a bachelor and wishing him luck and happiness. Their voices rose higher as they shouted, encouraging other bachelors to join in the holy bond of matrimony. Fatina chuckled at the scene. The name of the groom was graffitied on the wall of her neighbor's house, and it was surrounded by wishes and congratulations to "Mahmoud, the most handsome groom."

Fatina slammed her book shut, realizing that it was useless to attempt to study in that kind of atmosphere. On the far right, at the end of the wall, Fatina could still see traces of a previous graffiti that read, "Rest in peace, baby Mohammed."

Life and death were interlinked too closely for her to fathom. However, she also realized that even those most afflicted with pain made brave choices to persevere and carry on with life. Um Mohammed, who had lost her baby in the air strike that had mangled Fatina's hand, was already expecting another baby. Given the difficulty she had conceiving her first child, it was truly a miracle. Allah rewards those with patience, indeed. Upon hearing the news, all the neighbors went to congratulate Um Mohammed and pray that Allah would compensate for her loss with more babies to come.

FATINA

*Who and what we long to be are distant dreams.
I dreamed big, but somehow, someway, something
came in between. I grew up to learn that there
were dream robbers and dream killers. But God
sent me someone to keep my soul alive.*
—Fatina

Whether she was at school, at home, or walking down
the street, images of her future love flashed before
Fatina's eyes.

She always daydreamed about her future "knight
in shining armor" and what her future in Gaza would
be like. Something in the back of her mind told her
that this man would offer solace and comfort—that he
would wash away all her worries, and they would live
happily ever after. She tried to get over it.

Fatina came from Khan Younis, the second largest city in the Gaza Strip. Located in the southern part of the Gaza Strip, Khan Younis was home to one Palestinian refugee camp—Khan Younis Camp. Just five hundred meters away from the neighborhood was an Israeli military post called Mofaz Post—named after a former defense minister of the Israeli Army.

Fatina lived in that camp in a house made of bricks and a corrugated metal roof. This type of house absorbed extreme heat in the summer and cold in winter. Her home was one of a series of houses located in the city's narrow alleyways. A river of sewage water ran down the filthy dirt paths. The homes were built so close together that neighbors could hear each other quarrelling, talking over meals, washing dishes, and even flushing the toilet.

Deep inside, Fatina always detested the deplorable conditions of the camp where she grew up. She didn't want to spend the rest of her life in a refugee camp. Every day, she would lay on her bed contemplating her future. She had a habit of playfully curling strands of her pitch-black hair with her slim, delicate fingers. She did this when she was deep in concentration.

If Fatina had one advantage over the filthy living conditions, it was her captivating beauty. She was sure that one day it would be her ticket out of the camp she abhorred. In the camp where she lived, Fatina was disgusted by the unkempt and squalid way of living. Changing her life was beyond her reach, so planning to leave that kind of miserable life was the only thought on her mind.

Compared to the refugee camp where she and her family dwelled, other parts of Khan Younis seemed more livable. In the camp, she and her people were constantly reminded of their status as refugees with no decent place to call home. She'd often heard her grandparents saying that one day they would return to their hometown of Al-Majdal, but she couldn't grasp when or how that might happen. They would also boast about how many dunams of land they owned back home and how big their house was. All of this seemed to drive home the fact that the camp wasn't where she belonged.

Fatina's mother, Samira, was an overworked housewife, her hands gnarled from many years of hand-washing her family's clothes. Every washing day, Fatina saw wrinkles twisting in her mother's face as she wrung the clothes in a basin of soapy water.

As Fatina watched, Samira scrubbed shirts with cheap detergent that burned her skin. Next, she rinsed the shirts in a different basin that Fatina had filled with clean water. Then Samira twisted the clothes with all her might to rid them of excess water. Finally, Fatina took the clothes and hung them outside to dry.

Fatina took pride in her delicate hands and wanted to protect them. In the mental picture she had of her future, she didn't see herself doing any of those rough household chores.

One particular washing day, Fatina asked her mother, "Why can't we get one of those small washing machines? My friend Noor has one."

Samira continued scrubbing and rinsing, as if her daughter hadn't spoken. She wanted to respond, but she was too emotional. Since the day her husband, Jalal, had been shot, their lives had been turned upside down.

Since that day in 2002, life for Fatina's family had forever changed. It was two years into the Second Intifada. On that fateful day, Jalal was farming for a man who was originally from Khan Younis. The man owned around six dunams of land near the Israeli settlement of Gush Qatif.

Gush Qatif had nicer homes, parks, sporting facilities, and even potable drinking water that was supplied from the best wells in Khan Younis. It was nice enough that it could've been mistaken for a housing development in Europe or the United States.

Suddenly, four young men sprinted across one of the grape fields, taking shelter amidst the vines. The farmers saw them and shouted but couldn't locate them.

Shortly thereafter, the men emerged from their hiding place and ran until they reached the fence separating the farm from Gush Qatif. They quickly removed the large bricks used to conceal the small tunnel dug beneath the fence. In a matter of minutes, they had dropped to their bellies, slithered under the fence, and disappeared into the settlement.

Jalal could barely see what was happening from where he stood, but he heard the gunshots, and what sounded like a battle erupted. Three of the young men returned to the farm safely, and one of them was captured by Israeli soldiers. One Israeli settler was killed.

In retaliation, Israeli bulldozers ravaged the fields and razed some trees to the ground. Jalal saw an Israeli jeep coming toward him but didn't have time to take in what was happening. The jeep stopped midfield and a soldier got out and pointed his weapon at Jalal. In a flash, Jalal was shot in the left leg. Due to the severity of his injury, he ended up losing the leg.

All their lives, Jalal's family had been dependent on the United Nations Relief and Works Agency (UNRWA) for aid. Prior to losing his leg, Jalal's personal property was nothing more than a cart that he used for different purposes to make money and the mule that pulled it. But with Jalal no longer able to farm as a source of work, the UNRWA became their only source of food, including rice, lentils, dehydrated milk, and flour.

But such was life in a refugee camp. Fatina and her brothers tried to make the best of it, but even their school was dreary and lacking the most basic equipment. Spiderwebs hung loosely in the corners of the ceiling like dirty, tangled strands of hair from a witch's head. The dimly lit classrooms rendered the writing on the blackboard into hazy images that made the students strain their eyes to decipher. This deepened the dark circles already under their eyes from malnutrition. But Fatina survived it all. She managed to protect the twinkle in her eyes and keep it from dying out.

When Fatina graduated from high school, her parents couldn't afford to send her to college as she had hoped. She was nineteen, and she clenched her teeth in agitation every time she thought about it.

Although she acknowledged her family's destitution and desperately wished to rise above her circumstances, Fatina took pride in turning down all the good and bad men who proposed to her. She believed that her stubbornness would pay off one day, and her parents would eventually give in and find a way to enroll her at a college or university. Deep down, Fatina was fascinated by the idea of meeting different people at college—people from places other than the wretched camp she lived in. Going to college also meant that she would get the chance to travel for about forty minutes every day to the university located in Gaza City.

Samira and Fatina argued daily about marriage. But Fatina knew that if she succumbed to her mother's pressure to get married, she would lose any chance at having the life she was truly meant to live. Nevertheless, she was enchanted by the idea of a handsome man treating her like a queen, yet she was keenly aware that it would come at a price. And so, she rebelled against the idea of settling down with a husband and having children. From the time she'd been a young girl, one thing had been etched in her mind: She longed for the sweet taste of freedom, and that could only happen if she went to college.

Love

Beyond our visible stars and sky, there's another world waiting for us. A world of eternity where there's no toil, no pain, and no loss. My friend Omar was enchanted by the afterlife. He talked about it every day and dreamed about it every night. He wanted to get there. It was his most ardent wish.
—Abdullah

Just as death lurked behind every corner in the lives of those legendary Resistance fighters, so did love. Not a day went by when they didn't pour out their hearts to one another about their passions and their dreams. There was something sublime in the way they all had one thing running through their veins, something undisputed, one thing that eternally bonded their hearts and souls: their love of Palestine.

Abdullah and his comrades were on watch duty one night in the barren landscape of Khan Younis close to the fence separating Gaza from the rest of Palestine. Without the buzz of drones overhead, their heightened alertness was somewhat eased, relieving their minds for a while and allowing them to take in the tranquil, magical beauty of the sky.

"Omar," began Abdullah. "Was the human heart created to endure so much love?"

Omar kept his gaze on the magnificent display of moon and stars and said, "Not without so much heartache."

"When I think of how much I love this place, even with all its misery, I feel it may be incomprehensible to others. You know how it is when you fall in love, and your heart just hurts from the overflow of feelings? That feeling when you first meet the woman who will become your other half? The first look, the first kiss, and the first embrace where you feel you've found home?" Abdullah spoke softly, questioning and waiting for his friend to confirm his words.

Omar had a penetrating mind. At twenty-six years old, he was already commanding officer of his regiment. In only two years of working with Abdullah, Omar had become his friend, brother, father, and confidant. A precious bond united them and made their friendship unique in every way. And that bond was unbreakable. Still gazing at the stars, Omar spoke with a somber cadence, "No. Love of home is more entrenched.... It is mixed with our blood.

Our bodies are made from the same Palestinian soil. That's how I feel, but I don't know about your hugs and kisses," Omar turned his head toward Abdullah and gave him a sly smile.

Overcome with a sense of guilt, Abdullah put his head down and apologized, "Sorry man."

Omar had gotten engaged a month earlier, but after only two weeks, he'd decided to break it off. "It's OK. No need to be sorry. It was all a big mistake anyway. My parents thought she was right for me, and I gave in, thinking that's how marriages work. There was no spark, no magic, and no feelings. I felt as if I were a puppet with my family pulling the strings, so I acted in the way that pleased them and them only. But as you know, I was completely restless throughout the whole ordeal. Then one day I resolved to put an end to my misery, and I prayed and asked Allah to guide me to the right decision. And you know what happened that night?"

"What?" Abdullah stared in anticipation.

"I had the most beautiful dream of my life: I was sitting under the stars like we are now, and a door opened in the sky and a light shined down upon me. Its radiance was so powerful. My eyes squinted, but I forced them open. Then I heard the gentlest voice

I'd ever heard. It still rings in my ears. A woman was motioning with her delicate fingers as she called my name.

Her arm was bare and so white it seemed celestial. I followed the light, and as I approached, I heard more soft voices and sensual giggles. I ran and ran, following the light, but I woke up before I could grasp her hand!" Omar held his head with both hands in exasperation.

Abdullah sat dumfounded, yet the only thing he could think of saying was, "Have you told this to anyone?"—as if it were the most solemn secret.

"No, my friend.... You are the only one who will ever know," Omar assured him. "You see, I just feel that my *horeeyah* is up there waiting for me.... She called me by my own name. The sweet sounds of her voice and jingling bracelets still echo in my ears."

It was clear to Abdullah that his friend was in a trance and that he would seek that horeeyah for sure. On the outside, Omar the commander was a tough-skinned leader who had everything under control. His sense of responsibility was beyond idealistic. He suppressed his own emotions. He was like a rock, unruffled by anything that came his way. His altruism encompassed all those surrounding him. He was kindness personified.

As Abdullah listened to Omar's lonely speech, he knew deep down that Omar did not belong to this earthly place. He was an angel, and angels live in Heaven. The thought of losing him someday stung his heart, yet he wanted him to be happy, even if it meant him being with the horeeyah.

RESIST

April 2004

In my adolescence, I believed that love on Earth would be the solution to all my problems, like a magic potion that heals, connects, and revives the soul. But I found that I was selfish in my thinking. The love in Abdullah's heart extended to everyone and everything around him, but it all came at a price. I had to teach myself to be content with my share of him.

—Fatina

Time stood still.

Fatina was all alone in the apartment, but she still locked herself in her bedroom. Who she was hiding from she didn't know, yet she just felt the need to be alone. The huge volcano inside her was about to erupt.

She felt the need to hide from everyone and everything.

She looked at her bed and an eerie feeling flooded her. She felt weak, insignificant, and helpless. There was an enormous load weighing on her heart. It felt heavier than she could bear. She just sat on the floor. She needed something sturdy for support.

She leaned back against the closet, her head tilted backward. Before she knew it, suppressed tears streamed down her face and groans erupted from her heaving chest.

It was uncontrollable. She put her trembling fingers on her lips in an attempt to silence her cries but failed. An avalanche of thoughts ran through her overworked mind.

Her mind raced back to the first day that Abdullah had set eyes on her. She was captivated with his loving eyes and peaceful demeanor. For the first time in her life, she was entranced by a man.

He came to say he only wanted her.

Fatina was defeated for good. She surrendered.

A few moments of eternity passed. As they sat in her parents' living room that day, Abdullah said he had something important to say. He wanted to be honest with her. Fatina could hardly speak, but she managed to nod. She averted her eyes and fidgeted in her chair, trying not to reveal her awkwardness.

Abdullah sat back against the worn-out sofa. This slight movement revealed his bulging biceps through his neatly ironed, blue-striped shirt. A moment of silence passed. He caught her staring at him.

Abdullah stated the facts about who he was: "I just need to tell you that I have a passion." Their eyes locked for what seemed like an interminable period, then his face eased into a light smile and his tone softened into a whisper, "I am in the Resistance."

Abdullah searched her eyes for a response. Fatina sat up in her chair and tucked in a shiny strand of black hair that had fallen loose from beneath her emerald-green head scarf. If she stared long enough, she might have easily seen the reflection of her face in Abdullah's sparkling jade-green eyes. She blurted out, "That's beautiful."

The only thing Fatina felt was the heat burning her cheeks. She wasn't struck in the least bit. Her heart was in full control now; her mind was numb. The fact Abdullah had just revealed to her did not faze her.

Abdullah gazed at her not knowing how to respond. He grinned with rapture. Fatina seized her courage and probed, "Do you work in the tunnels?"

Abdullah was composed, but his heart beat rapidly. He inhaled deeply before replying, "I do different things."

That's how the freedom fighters always were, so silent about their duties. Fatina observed this from her brothers, who were also in the Resistance.

In the refugee camp where Fatina lived, many neighbors were in the Resistance. She often peeked through her window at night and watched them move about. She never saw their faces, and they all called each other by pseudonyms, like "Thunder" and "Lightning." But one night she overheard someone slip up and call out the name Ahmed. At that point, she realized that her neighbor Ahmed was in the Resistance.

She often pictured the freedom fighters as they fled into the night, and she wondered what they did out there while the rest of the city was in a deep slumber. She imagined them digging with their primitive tools, risking their lives.

The harsh facts were that every year dozens lost their lives in those dark tunnels. It didn't seem fair to her that young beautiful men who were in the prime of their lives dug in the dark to offer freedom to those living above. As they walked into the night, they seemed like giants who towered over her small world. She imagined that if she married one of them, he would take her with him into this world of midnight adventures. Yes, she would definitely fly away with him.

But here she was now with her aching heart and flood of tears. She was emotionally drained. She felt like a wrecked ship that had been hit by a ferocious storm. Her eyes burned badly from her salty tears, and a nasty headache was pulsating through her brain.

A year ago, she and Abdullah had both been sitting in her parents' living room in what seemed now a lost world of fanciful dreams. She let her heart lead that day when she gave her consent. Did she have any regrets now? Her heart and mind gave an unequivocal "No!"

She took solace from assuring herself that there were hundreds of women like her spending sleepless nights waiting for their husbands to come home. Or maybe they were stronger than her, and she was the only weak one. Or maybe those who had children busied themselves with taking care of them.

After they married, Abdullah had made Fatina's dream come true by enrolling her in college. She chose to study interior design—something she had always dreamed of. In fact, she was drawn to anything related to esthetics. Growing up, she often pictured her life outside the camp and imagined what her future home would be like.

Abdullah wanted her to keep busy, especially on those long days when he couldn't be with her. She cherished him for this and promised to love him forever. Tonight, she couldn't bring herself to study. Many nights she'd open a book and try to focus, but it seemed meaningless to her. Nothing made sense to her except scribbling their initials: *A + F.*

FANTASY

> *I never believed that the world of lovers existed*
> *in real life until Abdullah and I got engaged. It*
> *made me ponder how everything in life—no*
> *matter how beautiful—is transient. I often*
> *wondered just where eternal love existed.*
> —Fatina

Fatina and Abdullah's universe was at a standstill where no one, except them, existed. During their engagement when Abdullah came over to Fatina's house, her mother would knock lightly on the guest room door to serve them snacks or juice, but the food sat untouched.

Sometimes Abdullah would take her over to his family's house. Their neighborhood consisted of about 80,000 refugees coming from different parts of occupied Palestine, such as Isdod, Al-Jura, and Al-Madjal.

Abdullah's parents lived in a better part of the camp called Al-Amal, which was made up of real concrete houses with solid foundations, unlike Fatina's home with its punctured and cracked walls—not to mention the corrugated metal roof that allowed nocturnal rodents to trot back and forth over the heads of the family as they slept.

But the beach was Abdullah's and Fatina's favorite place to be. They went in the evenings and held hands while perched on a huge rock. They were content with this spot, which gave them solitude away from everything and everyone.

By the time they arrived, the beach was dark. But farther to the north they could see the illuminated port of Al-Majdal—one of the dozens of Palestinian cities whose citizens were displaced in the 1948 Nakba.

Whenever Abdullah proposed that they have dinner at a restaurant, Fatina would only agree if he took her to their rock afterward. Most of Gaza's restaurants were located along the beach and attracted a lot of people. Many had open areas where customers could eat and smoke.

So many young people smoked hookah to the point of suffocation. Fatina and Abdullah both felt alienated in that kind of atmosphere. They only felt their blue aura—a sense of peace and tranquility—when they were away from it all. Their special place gave them a rush of spiritual energy that healed their hearts and revved their souls yet numbed their minds. To Fatina, this was fantasy in its best form.

Their engagement had lasted only a month. Abdullah came to see her every single one of those thirty days. It was like they were both under a magic spell. During those thirty days, Fatina lived in the fantasy world of Disney princesses and princes falling in love. It was magical and surreal, yet she was very aware that it was transient. If only life had stopped there. If only "and they lived happily ever after" was true.

Fatina's friends were obsessed with soap operas. The constant euphoria mode of the lovers in those episodes had made sense to Fatina when she was younger, but it certainly didn't now. Her love for Abdullah permeated every part of her mind, heart, and soul and weakened her body with a relentless passion.

The wars that would break out, the earthquakes that might hit, or the tsunamis that could devour islands were all forbidden to enter her circle of concern. The mountains seemed weak compared to the insurmountable love in her heart. She was oblivious to all her surroundings. Abdullah alone was at the center of her world.

THE TUNNEL
WORLD

*When the whole world stigmatized my homeland,
we were forced to dig to find our way out of a life
under occupation and siege. It's hazardous work,
but we had no other choice. We were willing to
take the risk, yet it never occurred to me that
I might lose him.*
—Abdullah

Abdullah was barely aware of his comrades as they
dragged his near lifeless body and lifted it off the
ground. Slowly, sounds and images began to trickle
back. The sky was the first thing he saw when his eyes
flung open. It looked serene and soothing and was
in vast contrast to the turmoil that returned to his

awakened mind. He was relieved to inhale the fresh air, and his chest eased a bit.

Abdullah pressed his temples with his fingers in an attempt to recall something. That night, he had been more than sixty feet underground along with five other comrades. Small lanterns hanging on wires kept the tunnel dimly lit. The men dug with primitive equipment, shoveling dirt and piling it into wagons that were attached to a wooden track and pulled by power generators.

The tunnel reverberated with the clink and clank of iron against wood. The power generators sounded like roaring beasts that vibrated the ground and poisoned the air with toxins. No safety measures were taken in the tunnels. In fact, *safety* was practically a foreign word in the tunnels, where life was quite the opposite—hazardous.

Accidents were frequent and mostly deadly. Many involved tunnel collapses in which people were buried alive. Others met their end as they were being lowered down manually with a rope tied around their waists.

Inside the tunnels, the men used barrels cut in half and put as much sand in them as they could. Power cables attached to the barrels pulled them to the opposite end of the tunnel. The barrels were then lifted and emptied above the ground. Abdullah and all the others knew how dangerous this procedure was. Even the slightest accidental touch of the power line could get a man electrocuted, causing him to fall onto the track and get sucked under the wagons as if yanked by a giant cobra.

Abdullah worked eight hours with only short breaks in between. During those momentary periods of much-needed rest, his body would crash against the wall in exhaustion while he removed the cloth tied around his head to cover his nose and mouth. He would then use that same filthy cloth to wipe the dark streams of dirty sweat running down his fatigued face. His damp clothes clung to him like a stinky jellyfish, and for a second, he imagined the bliss of standing under a hot shower.

A friendly pat on the shoulder abruptly interrupted his thoughts. "Hey man," Ahmed called out as he plopped down next to Abdullah. Ahmed's comrades had dubbed him "the joker" because he was light-hearted and spirited and made everyone laugh.

"You know what, Abood?" said Ahmed.

"Yeah, what?" replied Abdullah as he leaned his head against the coarse wall.

"I think I'll get a nice mirror to hang up over here so you can see how hideous you look right now. I imagine your wife would scream in horror at the sight!" Ahmed laughed at his own sarcasm.

At the sound of the word *wife*, Abdullah saw Fatina's face illuminated before him. His heart raced at the thought of her slender arms surrounding him the minute he walked through their door.

"If only she could smell you—"

Abdullah cut him off, saying, "I assure you, buddy, that my wife loves me despite all my filth."

Someone nearby hollered to signal them to get back to work. Ahmed sprang up, "Come on, Abood," he said ruffling Abdullah's hair.

The men headed back to work, but Abdullah couldn't move. His muscles ached, and his head began pounding, heavily. He became short of breath and felt chills come over him. It was clear that he was coming down with a fever.

The sounds around Abdullah were beginning to drift away. Just then he heard the wagon coming to a halt, and soon his comrades would return to work. Abdullah didn't know whether he was awake or in a strange dream, but one thing was for sure—he was dead-tired. Suddenly, he lacked the strength to even lift his head, and his vision was getting increasingly blurry. The atmosphere in the tunnel was suffocating.

He saw shadowy movements as Ahmed operated the horrid power generator and began to pile dirt into the barrel. Ahmed's face looked hazy. Abdullah was beginning to hallucinate.

Ahmed's voice trailed off as he sang something to get his mind off the mechanical task he was performing.

Suddenly, Abdullah heard a horrifying scream and his heart thumped, yet he still couldn't move. A stomping of heavy boots accompanied earsplitting shouts. Someone screamed "Ahmed!" and the sound echoed in Abdullah's ears like a lion's roar.

All the sounds Abdullah had heard down in the tunnel suddenly seemed deafening, like a volcano was about to erupt within his head. Again, he heard someone screaming Ahmed's name.

Abdullah's head felt like it was spinning, his stomach churned, and his body perspired. Finally, he managed to lift his head. As he began to focus, he locked eyes with three of his comrades.

"Ahmed," Abdullah murmured, then he repeated in a louder but cracking voice, "Ahmed." He scanned the three pairs of eyes staring back sorrowfully. No one replied except Khaled, who was overcome by an outburst of sobbing. His shoulders shook uncontrollably. It didn't take long for Abdullah to realize what had happened.

Abdullah pulled himself up and flung himself at Khaled shouting profanities, "God damn you—all of you! You're nothing but beasts!" He lunged toward Khaled, balling up his fists to strike. But before he could make contact, Omar pulled him back. Abdullah continued, "Why'd you let me fall asleep? You killed him, you bastards. You killed him...."

Omar forced Abdullah to sit down then dug his fingers into his shoulders. "Abdullah!" he commanded. "Shut the hell up!" Their eyes were transfixed. Omar's muscles bulged, as if it took all his strength to maintain his control. "If you're gonna work in this hellhole, you gotta be a man. That means whatever happens, you gotta take it like a man. There are no other options, clear?" Abdullah's disheveled features tugged at Omar's heartstrings, so he softened his tone, "Say a prayer for him if you really love him."

Omar slowly loosened his grasp on Abdullah's shoulders and turned his head to hide his own grief.

In January of that year, seven Resistance fighters had drowned in a tunnel as heavy rains flooded the area. But today's tragic death was different. It would haunt Abdullah forever.

Rejuvenation

*I was amazed at how suddenly Abdullah
snapped out of his illness and devastation over
Ahmed. He lay sick in bed for two weeks, his
powerful body as weak as a child. He'd open his
eyes and look around, and then, realizing where
he was and what had happened, he'd sigh and
fall back into a turbulent sleep. When he was
finally back to his regular self, I felt that I'd
been born all over again.*
—Fatina

The whole neighborhood grieved Ahmed. It took every
iota of Fatina's physical and mental strength to absorb
the shock of what had happened.

Ahmed was the name she had overheard one of the
Resistance fighters call out one night as she stood at

her bedroom window in her family's home. He was her next-door neighbor and had been very popular with the children of the neighborhood.

When the young boys saw him coming down the street, piercing, excited voices would call out "Ahmed" as if a superhero had arrived. They would run to him and beg him to play soccer. He never let them down.

Even little girls would gather to take a piece of the candy that he brought—for the girls only.

All around the neighborhood, pictures showed Ahmed in his military uniform. His name was written in elegant calligraphy on walls, doors, and banners. After hearing the elders speak so proudly of Ahmed, the children fabricated stories about how he became a martyr:

"He was in the tunnel on his way to Jerusalem, and he had all these grenades," one boy said. "But when he reached the other end of the tunnel, there were many soldiers waiting, so he threw all the grenades, and BOOM! He killed a hundred of them and became a martyr."

"That's not how it happened," said another boy. "He was almost to Jerusalem and the Resistance fighters were waiting to fight with him. When he got there, they all started shooting at the Israeli soldiers—"

"No, that's not what happened!" another boy interrupted. "He went to Palestine, you know the other Palestine with all the Israelis—"

"What do you mean the other Palestine?" shouted another boy. "I'm gonna go ask my dad which Palestine we live in."

Following Ahmed's gruesome death in the tunnel, it took Abdullah two weeks to recuperate from the fever and hallucinations that had overtaken him that fateful day when his physical strength collapsed. Later, shock of Ahmed's death only made Abdullah's condition worse.

Normally, Abdullah's statuesque build seemed to tower over anywhere he stood. Now, for the first time, he was as feeble as a baby. He sought comfort by resting his head on Fatina's bosom.

Fatina and Abdullah seemed like trivial atoms trying to cling to God's power for security and assurance. Those moments of vulnerability really instilled in her the knowledge that Allah was the All Powerful and Almighty.

On the morning that Abdullah's ailments ended, he called out softly to Fatina, invigorated in body and soul. It was six o'clock in the morning. "Lulu, wake up," he said, giving her a peck on the cheek. "Come on. We're going out." Everyone else called her by the nickname Fefe, but to Abdullah she was his Lulu, which means pearl.

Fatina's eyes flung open in bewilderment. She could hardly make sense of what she'd heard. Abdullah was standing, fully poised, shaved, and dressed in casual dark blue jeans and a white T-shirt. She laughed and cried at the same time as she ran toward him, throwing her arms around his neck, "You're back!"

Abdullah engulfed Fatina in a long embrace. As he rubbed her back, he gently rested his chin on top of her head. Her lavender-scented shampoo filled his nostrils with nostalgia as her hot tears soaked into his T-shirt.

Between his mind and his body, Abdullah was filled with pent-up energy that he needed to release. The return of his physical strength took over, and he pushed away all attempts to talk. But as he held Fatina, he realized the toll his illness had taken on her. She'd grown thin, and her face was pale, "I'm sorry," he whispered. "But hey, we'll talk later. The beach is empty now. Let's go have some fun."

The beach was most peaceful in the early morning. It was a magnificent display of nature's beauty, where only the splash of waves and cries of seagulls could be heard.

Abdullah inhaled the salty morning breeze until his lungs filled with air. His senses were bringing him back to life. He turned and took Fatina in his arms, whirling her around with all his renewed energy. Her exhilarated screams only made him spin more vigorously until they both became dizzy and fell on the sand.

"Get back up," Abdullah said, pulling her to her feet. "Let's race!"

"That won't be fair!" Fatina pleaded.

"I'll give you a head start. But you better run fast because I'll be right behind you," Abdullah laughed flirtatiously. Without looking back, Fatina pulled up her *abaya* and ran away screaming with laughter.

After a few seconds, Abdullah was right on her tail, prompting her to scream even louder. Suddenly, she felt his arms sweeping her up like the sea waves.

"We both win, my love," he declared triumphantly.

BEAUTY

Abdullah's perception of beauty taught me to see the beauty within others. He urged me to notice the ordinary things in life that I'd taken for granted all my life. He helped me discover that the most beautiful things come from nature itself.
—Fatina

As a young Palestinian, Abdullah never had the chance to travel outside the Gaza Strip. But as a writer, he dedicated himself to describing his people's suffering and successes. He wrote about life in Gaza for websites and local and regional papers. He thought about traveling at times, but it seemed like a luxury or a distant dream.

Abdullah's mastery of the written word was impressive. Fatina was surprised when she first learned of his profession. She couldn't figure out how someone could be a writer and a Resistance fighter at the same time. To her, these two were an unlikely pair.

She was also fascinated at how Abdullah liked to keep his things in order. While dusting the desk—which she and Abdullah shared—she realized how contrary it was to what a typical man's desk looked like. Part of it held her college textbooks and notebooks. Another part had stationery and files where Abdullah kept all his work.

After their marriage, Abdullah tried to make her realize that writing was all about beauty. "As an aspiring interior designer, I know about beauty," she told him. "Beauty is the muse I'll use to design people's rooms so that they can showcase their artistic taste. It will enable me to help them express themselves through the colors and furniture they choose."

Fatina's interest focused on the physical beauty that she filled her world with, whereas Abdullah's was subtler. Fatina stood up and struck a pose. "You know what it means to me as a woman," she said, giggling as she tilted her head up high and ran her fingers through her lustrous raven-colored hair.

Abdullah leaned back on the sofa with his arms folded behind his head, contemplating Fatina's words. "So, according to your logic, my love, you have to be able to see and touch something for it to be beautiful?" he asked, smiling playfully. Although he disagreed with Fatina's view, he was certain that he could get her to agree with him in the end.

"Is this a quiz?" she answered. "Either way, my answer is yes." But the look in Abdullah's eyes suggested that it wasn't the answer he expected to hear.

Fatina liked to speak her mind, but she also didn't mind that Abdullah always seemed to have the right answers. Yet she felt a momentary sense of defeat and whined, "You have a way of making me feel like a schoolgirl, Aboodi (her most intimate nickname for Abdullah). Why can't I be right for once?"

Abdullah sprang up from the sofa, and took Fatina's hand, "Come on," he said leading her toward the balcony. "I'll give you a practical lesson."

Fatina followed suit. The small balcony overlooked the neighborhood mosque. There was an empty area of land beside the mosque where kids and teenagers played soccer. Far to the west, Israeli military outposts could be seen.

Fatina used the balcony to hang laundry to dry. She also had two potted plants that she attended to: mint and basil. Shortly after they were married, Abdullah asked her if she'd like to have a pair of lovebirds, but she rejected the idea completely. "I don't want to see two birds caged for my pleasure. I wish I could set all the caged birds free."

Her response had touched Abdullah, "Aw, *habibti*, you're so sweet. I never thought about it that way. Only someone who senses the true meaning of beauty would say that." As Fatina recalled that conversation, she thought that maybe he might change his mind about her concept of beauty.

Abdullah stood behind Fatina with his arms wrapped around her waist. He urged her to look up at the magnificent stars in the sky. "Can you see any beauty up there?" he whispered into her ear.

"I feel your warm breath tingling down my spine," Fatina giggled. It was the first time she'd ever contemplated the sky, and the splendid beauty she beheld captivated her. "It's breathtaking."

Was it the way he leaned his head against her right temple as he whispered softly? Or had she simply never noticed the sparkle of the stars and the serenity of the sky before? Perhaps it was both.

"See, if you meditate on it long enough, the stars and moon will speak to you. This is nature's gift of beauty that we can watch and enjoy for free every night, but we don't."

Abdullah spoke in a slow assured voice that made Fatina turn her head and stare at him as if he were speaking some kind of mystical language.

"My friend Omar agrees with me. At night, when we're on watch duty, we sit under the stars and they blink at us. We see faces in the moon; sometimes they're happy faces, sometimes they're sad. But trust me, sweetheart, nature is the most magnificent of Allah's creations, and nature gives you peace. Your furniture and interior designing are artistic, but there's nothing like the universe that God has created. Right here in Palestine, there are enchanting landscapes, forests, and beauty that will make you feel like you're in Heaven."

Fatina felt as if she were under some kind of spell. "Abood," she whispered as she pulled him into a warm embrace. "You're a magician."

A Special Operation

Omar had made up his mind. He wanted to
go be with his love in Heaven. I couldn't stand
in his way, so I gave in. Omar was longing for
something beyond our human reach. We spent
long nights preparing every meticulous detail of
the operation together, but a battle was raging
inside me. I wanted the mission to succeed, but
I wanted Omar to return safely.
—Abdullah

Like a film that he'd seen too many times, images
played over and over in Abdullah's mind, evoking an
anger that was boiling up to the surface. Like other
Palestinians, Abdullah had been born into a world
where Ariel Sharon's military exploits brutalized

Palestinians. The only world Abdullah knew was one of Israeli occupation, murder, imprisonment of family members, and deadly air strikes that shattered houses, buildings, and people. Israeli soldiers in warplanes and Apache helicopters slaughtered Resistance fighters and assassinated political figures. Drones bombed neighborhoods and government buildings in a modern mode of warfare and collective punishment. The bombings created sudden sonic booms that, like an earthquake, rocked entire neighborhoods and villages—people, animals, buildings, trees, and everything in between.

What Abdullah and his comrades had planned for retribution they considered a debt owed to the widowed women, orphaned children, imprisoned youth, and mutilated Palestinians. At one o'clock on a Saturday morning, Abdullah and his battalion were underneath the city of Rafah in the southern Gaza Strip. This would be the day that would make the world stop turning. The whole world would be talking about it.

On the day of the operation, emotions were running high and hearts pounded with anticipation. The men invoked Allah, holding their hands up in supplication.

The operation had taken weeks of planning; the men had been calculating their moves and carrying out maneuvers to ensure precision. Being fully alert was the key to their success, and they practiced it every day using different techniques. They also adhered to a strict diet and exercise program. Omar, their commanding officer, ordered them to eat specific brain-boosting foods to enhance their cognitive abilities. Omar also had them complete drills, and he showed no mercy toward anyone who made the slightest fumble.

It was after practicing one of these drills that an unfortunate soldier named Khalil was scolded in front of his comrades for his unsatisfactory performance. His lack of focus and precision was noticeable.

Omar planted his hands on the table in front of Khalil and faced him with icy eyes and a venomous tone. "Being part of the Special Operations Unit is no joke. Every move you make must be precisely calculated. There is no room for even a minor slipup. You eat and drink only what is on the list. You do not exert yourself with any unnecessary physical activities on exam night, and that includes … I'll try to put this as delicately as possible.…" Omar said. His face was stern and stony in a way that made his jawbones protrude at the sides. He averted his gaze to a nearby window, cleared his throat, and lowered his voice. All ears in the room strained to hear what they already guessed. "Ahem … staying away from marital relations just like athletes are required to do before an important game." It took a tremendous amount of energy for Omar to maintain his composure and keep a solemn expression on his face while saying that.

Omar continued, "Something you may not know about me is that I can recognize stupidity when I see it. And in your case, soldier, it's written all over your face!" Listening to Omar's reprimand, everyone in the room stood as still as statues.

Omar was infuriated. He stood tall with his chest puffed up like a dragon, ready to unleash his wrath and blow fire on his victim.

As Khalil stood there in humiliation, a wave of blood flushed his face, reddening his cheeks. "Sir—" he said in a useless attempt to speak.

Omar cut him off instantly, "Silence! You are dismissed from the training program." Omar did not budge from his spot. From his stationary position, he ordered the rest of the trainees to leave—except Abdullah.

As Omar's deputy officer, Abdullah was responsible for following up on the training. "I assure you that Khalil was the only one who gave an unsatisfactory performance. We can begin the maneuvers for week four of the training. It will take forty-eight hours."

Omar walked to the window and rested his hands on the windowsill. Abdullah sensed something important coming. "Is everything OK, Omar?"

"Abdullah, you're going to lead this operation from A to Z," Omar replied in a calm and controlled tone.

Abdullah was taken by surprise, "But you are the commanding officer, Omar."

Omar scrutinized Abdullah's eyes before he announced, "I've received orders from the top commander. I'm going under."

Abdullah tried to maintain his calm, but his facial expressions failed him. His pupils dilated and his eyebrows furrowed as his mind tried to fathom the enormity of what he had just heard. His dear friend had decided to participate in the perilous mission. "Is this negotiable?"

"I've made up my mind, and I won't back down," Omar said with confidence.

ONE NIGHT

*In the blink of an eye, my whole life was turned
upside down. When the attack happened, it
occurred to me how—in a split second—one's life
can change forever. I was in a daze. Was I dead
or alive? I did not know. My mind was drifting to
another world where I was screaming for Abdullah,
but he couldn't hear me. My voice was being suppressed by another power. A scary, scruffy man was
chasing after me. Panting, I ran and ran to escape,
calling Abdullah. Before this, whenever I had
nightmares, he always woke me up and held me
tight. But this time, he was nowhere to be found.*
—Fatina

Once the Second Intifada broke out in September 2000,
deadly air and artillery strikes began to wreak havoc
and horror across the Gaza Strip. Most nights when

there were strikes, Fatina would cling to Abdullah like a frightened child. All she needed was to hear his reassuring voice as he wrapped her in his arms, "It's all right, habibti. Nothing's gonna happen. I'm here." That was enough to soothe Fatina and dispel her fears. Abdullah was her superhero. At times, she was ashamed of her childish behavior, yet she still retreated to him for protection and security.

One day, she rebelled against her own feelings and whined, "You always say it will be OK, but I know you only do that to appease me." Although her tone was defiant and accusing, she still waited for his usual calming words.

"I swear, Lulu. Those warplanes have already taken out their targets. I just heard it on the news."

Fatina's heartbeat dropped to a normal speed, but her mind continued to race. Still fearful, she asked, "Abdullah, how do they know who's in the car?"

"From the damn traitorous spies who I pray will burn in life and death!" Abdullah spouted angrily. "Those traitors put a fluorescent chemical on their palms then touch the car they want bombed. The pilots in the planes detect this chemical and shoot."

Fatina's eyes widened, and her heart thumped as, once again overwhelmed by fear, she pleaded, "Abdullah, please don't ride in any cars."

Later, while Abdullah was at his night shift and Fatina was studying—examining an equation on measuring dimensions, which required her complete concentration—she heard an Israeli F-16 warplane roaring above. Then it was gone.

That night in bed, Fatina held a notebook in her lap and one of her textbooks by her side. Writing out anything she needed to memorize helped her stay focused. She knew from experience that staring into a book without involving her other senses would either cause her mind to wander to wherever Abdullah was or make her fall asleep.

She listened to see if the fighter jet would come back. She tried to dismiss the thought and attempted to focus on her schoolwork. The last thing she needed was to think about something bad happening to her while she sat at home all alone.

But then suddenly, the sound of several warplanes invaded the night, shattering the silence in the apartment. Israeli F-16s were shelling the neighborhood.

As soon as she heard the planes, Fatina immediately leaped out of bed and tried not to panic so she could think clearly. Her first thought was to wrap herself in any garment and run downstairs to her in-laws apartment. She was thankful that other people lived in the same building.

But the warplanes zoomed overhead at supersonic speeds, faster than the thoughts that raced through her agitated mind. Before Fatina even had time to react, three deafening blasts rocked the building. But before she could even open her mouth to scream, the window across the room exploded. A torrent of shattered glass sprayed in her direction, as if machine guns were pelting the room. Thrown against the door by the force of the explosion, she fell in a crumpled heap to the ground, unconscious.

In the aftermath of the attack, Fatina struggled to make sense of what had happened. She tried not to overreact, but she needed to process her emotions: Where was Abdullah? Did she resent him for not being there with her that night? Why had he always promised that everything would be all right? And could she really blame him, or should she blame herself for being naive? The biggest question looming on her mind was: Could she ever love herself again after the permanent injury she'd sustained?

The night of the Israeli bombardment, as shattered glass was blown in her direction, a piece of shrapnel pierced her hand and tore through the tissue. Her soft elegant skin was deformed forever.

The deformity stirred up feelings of depression and self-pity. Fatina couldn't stop thinking about all the household chores she had once refused to do just to protect her slim fingers and long nails. Now, her hand became something repulsive that she had refused to accept as her own.

But she reasoned with herself to keep Abdullah out of the intrusive thoughts that poisoned her mind. Instead, she chose to have different conversations with herself. *I know I love him, and nothing could ever change that. He doesn't stay out all night with his friends playing cards or watching soccer. No. He has a purpose in mind—a very noble cause.*

She remembered how one day, as they sat on their rock, she'd teased him about being in love with another woman.

"It's no use, habibi; you can't fool a woman. Women are sharp-witted creatures. I know her name." Fatina tried not to sound serious, although her innermost emotions were mixed.

Amused by Fatina's insinuation, Abdullah chuckled and questioned playfully, "Is that so, my brilliant lover? Have you found any evidence in my belongings?"

"No, but it's in your eyes when you talk about her and the way you describe her perfect features. I must confess, I'm jealous. But I guess I'll just have to share you and settle for being a second wife ... since *she's* your first.

That night, they watched the magnificent sun as it sank beyond the horizon to rise in another part of the world. Abdullah drew Fatina closer into his expansive chest and whispered, "You're my first and my last, Lulu.… And that other one … I know you love her as much as I do. She's in your blood and soul, and we are both intermingled with her. I wouldn't have married you if you were from another soil."

Fatina wondered if the uphill battle inside her head existed for other Palestinian women. Or did they go about their lives in an ordinary fashion? She knew she wasn't alone, but that didn't provide her with the consolation she needed most—at least not yet. The tug-of-war inside her head would continue until she made up her mind to accept her reality with all its good and bad.

Hasna

*She visited me in my sleep. Her voice was like
nothing I'd ever heard from any woman on
Earth. In the dream, I ran to her; I chased her.
But she was too far away to be reached. She
knew my name and reached out her celestial
hand to give me something. I held out my hand
and grabbed it. What I wanted even more was
to hold her hand.*
—Omar

As the city was engulfed in darkness and late sleepers
slumbered in their warm beds, Omar stood under the
stars watching the border. He was the firm commander
whom everyone revered. He shouldered his duties with
steadfast devotion and could never be swayed to give
up on something he ardently believed in. The most

belligerent enemy could hardly shake him. He stood uncontested, unrivaled, and unbreakable.

By looking at Omar's erect posture and assured manner, a stranger might have perceived him as haughty. He moved with boldness and defiance, as if ready to move a mountain with his finger. Violent sea waves and the stealthiest snake would retreat from his monumental presence. His source of power lay in his sagacity—his keen sense of perception and attentiveness to minute details. He never faltered, never hesitated, and certainly never questioned the nobility of his duty.

Omar's shift ended at midnight. Before leaving, he took one last glance at the sky and allowed himself to take in the beauty of the night. His eyes were trans-fixed skyward as if summoning a divine spirit. Since the dream, he hadn't been the same. A deep yearning plagued him with insomnia. He ached with nostalgia.

On a rare occasion when Omar's weary body sur-rendered to sleep, he saw her again in a dream. A sweet delicate symphony called out his name. His body was electrified as he searched frantically to find her. He turned around, answering, "Yes, yes!" without seeing her face. "Where are you? Please talk to me."

Omar strained his ears, desperately trying to hear her. Suddenly, amidst harmonious jingling a melo-dious voice addressed him in an solemn tone saying, "Take this."

Stupefied, Omar held out his trembling hand to take hold of the glowing rifle she handed him. His firm grip on the metal circulated energy down his spine. Afraid to see her vanish, Omar cried out, "Please, tell me your name! Please!"

As a sweet, angelic laugh penetrated his ears, Omar bolted up from his pillow, panting for breath. The voice echoing in his ears sounded so real that he sprang out of bed and turned on the light to see who was there. Recognizing his surroundings, Omar switched off the light, leaned his back against the door, and inhaled deeply. "Hasna ... I'm coming, Hasna. I promise."

Another voice brought Omar back to reality. Before he knew it, the *Fajr* call to prayer awakened him at dawn, breaking the silence in his room. He listened to the *muezzin* call out the prayer with rapture, and he repeated after the incredible voice, *"Allahu Akbar."*

Loss

They say there is no greater pain than the loss of a loved one. Although I believed this to be true, what I lost on that dreadful night was almost as horrifying ... my loss was nearly as difficult to overcome. I lost my peace of mind, my stability, my confidence, and my zest for life. My neighbor lost her only child; my loss was almost as painful.
—Fatina

After a long day at school, Fatina retreated to the peace and solitude of her small apartment—her own personal paradise. But on the night of the bombing, her tranquil abode had been shattered like the glass in her window. Fatina couldn't stop thinking about the foreboding silence that preceded the Israeli air strike. Since then, the stillness of her home was like a ferocious monster lurking and preparing to attack without warning. Fear constantly rippled through her bereaved heart. And she dreaded both solitude and silence.

Her neighbors' eight-month-old baby, Mohammed, had been killed during the bombing. The infant had been conceived after a ten-year journey of fertility treatments and medication. During that decade, Um Mohammed's struggle to conceive was a frequent topic of the gossip that circulated throughout the camp. The pity and judgment of her neighbors only added to Um Mohammed's misery over her inability to conceive a child.

Nonetheless, Um Mohammed and her husband never gave up hope. She willingly sold all her gold jewelry to pay for the necessary treatments in the hope of fulfilling her maternal instincts.

To her bliss, it all paid off. All the pain she had experienced during those long ten years instantly vanished when she first gazed into her baby's eyes and caressed his tiny cheeks. But only eight months later, when her baby's life was snuffed out in a flash, Um Mohammed was once again the recipient of her neighbors' pity— the epitome of the accursed and heartsick, crushed, devastated, and broken beyond repair.

Fatina's loss, too, was tragic. She was shaken to the core of her being. Did she not have the right, like Um Mohammed, to retreat into and wallow in her sorrow?

Some would say she was acting like a child, but what right had they to judge her? When Abdullah attempted to remind her that it wasn't as if she had lost a child, she rebuffed him defiantly with a frigid, "I know that."

Fatina abandoned all efforts to keep up with her housework—and worse—her marriage. Abdullah felt that their small place was gradually collapsing and none of his methods were working anymore. When Fatina developed a phobia of being home alone, Abdullah knew he needed to get her some help.

Whenever Abdullah returned to their apartment, Fatina was nowhere to be found. One day she'd be at her parents' house; the next she'd be at her in-laws' place. Sometimes, she would just spend the entire day at the university, and at the end of the day, if Abdullah wasn't at home, she would go somewhere else.

Fatina's mood swings exasperated Abdullah to the point that he thought fighting his enemy at the border was easier than his struggle at home. None of his usual techniques to cajole Fatina proved effective, so Abdullah decided to try something new.

METAMORPHOSIS

My father would always say that behind every calamity, there's a blessing. After the bombing, I tried to find the good in the tragedy that had happened. It's true that I survived, but my injury was too visible to forget. I was tormented mentally. Eventually, I found myself transforming into a new person—someone who cared about things I had never noticed before.

—Fatina

The attack had left her visibly scarred for life. Shrapnel from the exploding Israeli bomb had mangled her delicate hand, leaving it an eyesore that was impossible to forget. Her disfigurement made her terribly self-conscious and anxious wherever she went. It was like being stabbed to death in the heart. It was a conspiracy.

As Fatina walked down the street, she felt the buildings and houses closing in on her. Even the cars seemed to vent their anger at her with their incongruous horns. When she got home, the sense of relief that washed over her was fleeting. It was as if she'd just escaped from a monster. But soon, the whole scene would repeat itself in a different way.

Even something as simple as opening her closet to pick something to change into was tainted. Her taste in clothes had always been refined, and she took pride in the way anything she wore perfectly fit her body. But now all those garments looked like worthless material. They did nothing to elevate her mood.

Abdullah loved to see her wear light colors because he loved the way they contrasted magically against her bronze-colored skin and jet-black hair. Before her injury and the subsequent depression, she felt like a special bond existed between herself and every item of clothing she bought. Any dress she wore accentuated her beauty. But now she no longer felt attached to any item. And certainly not to light colors. She wore her cool black hoodie most days because she felt that dark colors helped her hide herself. The same was true with her accessories, which were suddenly plain and meaningless to her. She thought about just giving them away. It seemed silly to her now that an object, such as an accessory or article of clothing, could make anyone happy.

Fatina no longer believed in the way people perceived happiness, for even happy occasions ceased to make any difference in her life. At family celebrations, she had always been the star. Now, she withdrew herself from those occasions because, deep down, they only added to her sense of loss and desperation. In fact, sad occasions were the only reality she acknowledged because they were where people revealed their true selves and talked sensibly about mortality.

The injury also made her notice the wretched ones who suffered varying plights. She hated the way people looked down on others. Where she lived, a young worker came to pick up the garbage every morning. As he did his job, he would recite some verses of Quran or sing a religious song. Fatina no longer saw his dirty hands; she only heard his beautiful voice.

Um Mamdouh, an old woman in her early sixties who lived down the street, would greet Fatina on her way out. Before, Fatina always smiled at her from a distance, but now she stopped to shake the old woman's calloused hand. The woman was tidy, but she wore an over-sized embroidered dress that she may have gotten from one of her sisters.

Fatina felt a new force inside drawing her to these people with whom she could relate as a result of their shared suffering. Everyone suffered under Israeli occupation in their own unique way. Fatina's reasons for suffering may have seemed trivial compared to others, but it nevertheless affected her deeply.

Sugar

I had to dig deep in my mind to find something that would redeem Fatina. She loved tangible beauty, but nothing I could buy would mean anything to her in her current state of mind. Then I remembered something she always sketched in her notebook. I realized this just might be the remedy.
—Abdullah

Abdullah grew weary of the trauma Fatina was experiencing, and his hatred toward the Israeli occupation only intensified. The idea of warplanes bombing civilian neighborhoods with the press of a button outraged him.

"If they were real men, they'd fight on the ground." He often said this when he talked with his comrades. Alamal, his neighborhood, was blighted with misery at the beginning of the Second Intifada. Abdullah's brother had been killed in the course of the fighting, and his cousin Mohammed lost both of his legs in a car bombing. Mohammed wasn't even the target; he was simply a passerby. That didn't matter, though, because everyone nearby got hurt—collateral damage they called it. And now, with the specter of Israeli aggression threatening his wife, Abdullah's fury escalated, "I swear, they will pay for their savage crimes," he vowed.

Trying to reason with Fatina through her cycle of loss proved fruitless, so Abdullah reverted to something he was sure would help her snap out of it.

"Lulu," Abdullah whispered as he pushed back the strands of hair covering her eyes. It was one of those mornings when Fatina slept late. Sleep had become her way of escaping life's burdens of fear and anxiety.

But Fatina didn't respond. On other days, the moment she heard Abdullah's comforting voice, her senses were instantly brought back to life. To her, there was nothing more melodious than his voice, but on this particular day, she was oblivious to his presence altogether. She simply rolled over and pulled the covers over her head.

Abdullah wasn't about to give up, "You know what time it is?"

"I don't care," she murmured.

"I know you don't care, but I still do. That's why I have a surprise for you."

"I've had enough surprises," she replied flippantly.

"No, this is the best surprise. It's something you've always wanted to see and hold," Abdullah continued. He was hopeful now that she would take the bait.

"Where is it—this thing?" she asked.

"It's not here. But come on, get up. I'll take you there." Abdullah exhaled in relief that his plan was working. He wanted to be the one to break Fatina's cycle of depression and fear, and he prayed that she would succumb and allow him to heal her.

She lifted the covers and sat up with her elbows on her knees and her hands half covering her face. "Not into one of your tunnels, I hope. I know I used to beg you to take me. How stupid of me!"

Abdullah sighed and put his arms on Fatina's trembling shoulders. "You're so mean to me, Lulu," he said calmly. "Why would I do that? I'd never want you to see the darkness down there. No, you were born to see and touch beauty like yourself. And that's the surprise I've prepared for you. I promise, you'll love it. If you don't, you can slap me as hard as you can."

When they reached the beach, it was almost noon. Fatina let go of Abdullah's hand and threw herself on the sand; she was already growing warm in the sun.

She glanced at Abdullah. "I'm already tired," she said with a yawn. She took off her shoes and dug her toes into the sand. She loved the way it tickled her feet.

"OK. Close your eyes, and don't turn around or peek," Abdullah said with feigned excitement. This was his last plan, so it had to work.

The Gaza beach was the place that held the most cherished moments for Abdullah and Fatina. To them, it was magical. He trusted the waves, the seagulls, and the sand to work their magic and bring Fatina back to him.

"Open your eyes," Abdullah called out.

With her toes still buried, numbed by the tingling sensation of the sand, Fatina lifted her head slowly. She furrowed her eyebrows and stared in disbelief. There, right in front of her, was the most beautiful horse she had ever seen.

"Come on. Let me introduce you to Sugar," Abdullah said excitedly.

Fatina's face lit up as she walked over to the horse. Extending her hand slowly, as if she was about to touch something sacred, she stroked the horse's blonde mane. Running her hand over the horse's coat, she could feel its strength.

"Abdullah, she's beautiful," Fatina cried softly. She put her arms around the horse's neck and rested her head lightly against it. The horse was calm.

"Hey, I think she likes you," Abdullah cheered.

Fatina didn't lift her head. She just pulled her arms closer around the horse's neck and said, "She's both stunning and strong." Those words touched Abdullah's heart because that's how he wanted Fatina to be again—strong. He wanted her to conquer her fears even if she could only learn to do so from a horse.

"You know, Lulu, I think you're gonna learn a lot from Sugar. She'll teach you how to become invincible."

"How can I learn from her when I don't know the first thing about riding a horse?"

"That's about to change, my love," Abdullah assured her. "You have your very own personal—and may I add, handsome—trainer."

Abdullah could finally feel his heart easing as he saw the spark of life light up Fatina's eyes. There were still dark circles beneath them, but the way her face shined with excitement and happiness made the darkness vanish. Abdullah was beaming as Fatina stood hugging the horse tighter. "I'm already jealous of Sugar. How come she gets all the hugs?"

Suddenly, a pang of guilt overtook Fatina. She had been pushing him away for such a long time. He looked like an abandoned child. Lately, she'd rebuffed any attempts Abdullah had made to get near her, hold her, or be intimate in any way. Fatina felt like a cranky old phone that refused to pick up any signals. And to add insult to injury, Fatina's bony and malnourished figure made her look like a ghost or an old witch. That's how she perceived her new self. "So, when do we start our lessons?" she asked.

"Right now!" he exclaimed. "But you gotta hold on tight or you'll fall. And if you seriously want to learn to ride Sugar, you need to start getting back into shape. You know, to put some meat on those bones."

"OK, Mr. Cute Trainer. I'll start behaving," she conceded.

It was a warm spring afternoon with a crisp breeze that caressed Fatina's cheeks. Abdullah mounted the horse first, then he pulled Fatina up, and she held him tightly. He pulled the reins and Sugar trotted steadily, then cantered along the beach as if heading for the horizon.

Fatina closed her eyes and embraced the excitement whirling inside her—a feeling she had missed for so long. She wished that she and Abdullah could vanish into the world she knew only existed in her imagination—a world where people weren't killed by warplanes, a world where people didn't have to wake up to the smell of blood and the sight of rubble and smoke. If only Sugar would take them to some faraway land, beyond all the madness of life under occupation.

No Joke

*My passion kills me sometimes. I may go to
extremes to defend what I love and what I
believe in. Sometimes it's hard to accept the
other side of the argument. But when I put
myself in other people's shoes, I begin to understand the way they think. I cherish Abdullah
and his role in the Resistance, but it's clear that
there are others who don't.*
—Fatina

One evening while Abdullah was on duty, Fatina was
at her parents' house when two of her cousins and an
aunt stopped by to visit. They sat outside in a small dirt
space where some mint and basil plants were growing.
The two cousins, Anwar and Salah, were smoking their
hookah pipes and telling tasteless jokes—the kind that
only exist in men's minds.

They kept their voices low, but every few minutes, Fatina heard laughter erupt. They never tired of their jokes, but Fatina was sick of hearing them, so she decided to go inside. Fatina also wanted to escape her aunt's intrusive questions about having babies and whether Abdullah's mother made her do housework for her and other details that she always avoided by being evasive.

When Fatina returned with a tray of tea and cookies, Salah and Anwar were making gestures at each other. Anwar exhaled a long puff of smoke and turned toward Salah, "Hey Salah," he raised his voice to exaggerate his question. "Those tunnel men...."

"What about them?" replied Salah.

"Do you think they have tunnel women down there?" Then, suddenly, Anwar burst out laughing at his own joke, and Salah gave a shriek, rocking back and forth to contain himself.

Fatina felt her cheeks burning. If it had been daytime, everyone would've seen her red-hot face about to explode like an overripe tomato. She felt fire in her eyes and was about to lash out without mercy. Samira, Fatina's mother, and the aunt seemed oblivious to what was being said. Fatina knew her cousins' insinuations were meant for her, and she was determined to pay them back instantly.

Fiery words flew from her mouth like lava spewing from a volcano. Her brain wasn't in control, only her tongue. "If you two pigs don't shut up, I'm gonna shove that hose you're smoking down your throats so hard that your intestines will ooze out of your mouths like a slaughtered sheep."

The two men froze. Samira and her sister-in-law looked bewildered, but Fatina continued. "If you want to make sick jokes, this isn't the place to do it."

Samira rose and tried to calm her daughter. "Fatina, these are our guests and—"

"Mother, you didn't hear what they just said."

"We were only joking, cousin," Anwar replied, feigning remorse.

"Yeah. Why did you take it so personally? Why do you care about the tunnel men anyway? They work in filth all day and night," Salah chimed in.

Was that how her cousins perceived Abdullah and the others? Fatina couldn't believe what she was hearing. Even though almost everyone she knew worshipped those in the Resistance, she realized that there were others who were demeaning and believed the work of the freedom fighters was insignificant.

Fatina couldn't hold back her anger. "You are a gruesome weasel! Shut up and get out of here! And as for your tea—" she picked up the cups forcefully and poured the tea across the ground. "It's gone. Those men you speak of so lowly are more honorable than you will ever be. You get to put your head on your pillow every night and probably watch filthy movies. Those men are out there protecting the city so you can sleep peacefully. But how can someone like you even understand what that is like!"

Fatina's aunt was outraged, and Samira did everything she could to appease her. "Fatina, apologize to your cousins," she ordered.

But Fatina would have no part of it. "Me apologize? Not until they take back every word they said." Fatina watched her two cousins. Unlike her, they actually seemed amused by the whole scene. They weren't as vehement about what they'd said as Fatina was. In fact, it appeared that they took delight in causing such an uproar.

"Hey cousin, we're only saying that they waste themselves down there and get themselves killed for nothing. That's simply my point of view. Aren't I entitled to my opinion? Why can't you accept the way others think?"

At that moment, Anwar's words struck Fatina, and she felt a pang of guilt, for there was truth in them. But she still felt the need to defend herself—and her husband. "I'll respect what others think if they present it in a respectful manner, not in the way you have."

"OK, fair enough. But you *do* know we were only joking, right? You sure got carried away defending them, though," Anwar said, gazing at her, trying to read what she was hiding. Anwar suspected that Fatina's brothers were in the Resistance, but he knew nothing about Abdullah's clandestine activities. It's likely he had no doubts after the lashing he and Salah just received.

Fatina was tired and didn't wish to continue the conversation. Her emotions were stirred up enough, so she decided to call a truce. "Does this mean you want to apologize now?"

Salah didn't like her suggestion, so he retorted, "We didn't hurt you! We were talking about other people, cousin."

He had Fatina backed into a corner, but she wasn't about to let him enjoy the victory or get her to admit that Abdullah was part of the Resistance. "You insulted the men of our neighborhood, and I won't stand for that."

Salah took a long drag on his pipe and mumbled, "OK, OK. We're sorry we disrespected the work of our courageous men. But can you convince me that they're doing an honorable and worthy job?"

Fatina thought it would only be appropriate to apologize too since she'd promised, so she muttered, "I'm also sorry."

Her cousins had put her on the spot, so she quickly had to prepare a speech in her head to defend what she believed was honorable but was also something that she was struggling to fully accept as her reality. Could she really defend the freedom fighters? She needed to come to terms with the fact that she *was* a firm believer in what her husband chose to do and what he chose to be.

"It's simple," Fatina began. "Just like in other countries—where people honor and look up to soldiers, police officers, and firefighters, we have to do the same with the freedom fighters."

Anwar and Salah became quiet and solemn. It was hard to believe that they were the same two who were making jokes moments before. "But Fatina, the people of Palestine have been suffering for decades," Salah continued. "Thousands have been martyred, I can't say there have been any tangible benefits to this armed struggle."

"So, if the occupation continues to kill our people, are we supposed to just lie down and take it, rationalizing that resisting and defending ourselves would be useless? Come on, what kind of logic is that?" Fatina countered.

Anwar was stimulated to join the conversation and defend Salah's point of view. "I say those who want to resist can do so, but the others who can't or don't want to shouldn't be admonished for that. I mean, in the end, not everyone is a fighter. Am I right?"

Fatina nodded her head in agreement, realizing the truth in her cousin's words: Not everyone was going to be a fighter. There would always be some who chose not to fight, and their roles were just as important.

Deep down, Fatina still refused to feel sorry for being defensive about what she believed to be true. But she also needed to accept other people's points of view.

A BABY

In my hometown, after marriages take place,
couples instantly start thinking about having
children. With no exotic plans to travel for a
honeymoon, there's a limit to what they can do.
I tried to push that issue away in an attempt to
do more adventurous things, but then the time
came to get realistic.
—Fatina

Fatina's and Abdullah's second wedding anniversary was approaching, and both of their families began to ask why they weren't having babies. Fatina was so caught up in her coursework at the university and enjoying her lessons with Sugar that she didn't even want to think about a baby tying her down. When Abdullah brought up the subject, she spoke her mind bluntly. "Abood, you know that I can barely take care of myself. I can't imagine being responsible for another human being." She paused before asking, "Does that make me an abnormal wife?"

In his mind, Abdullah replayed all the events of the past two years. He knew too well that he had to deal with this sensitive subject differently than the rest of the family did. "You know, darling, I don't want to pressure you. You've certainly had more than your share of that recently. But I often wonder, if we had a little girl how much she would take after you."

Fatina's facial features relaxed, and she found herself laughing. "So, you want a girl first?"

"If she's gonna have your eyes, then yes, I would," Abdullah cooed.

"And what would you name her?" Fatina asked curiously.

Abdullah's eyes twinkled with love. It was a look that always took Fatina back to the moment when their eyes first met. Abdullah got that look when he was about to say something that would make Fatina smile. "There's only one name in the world I'd call her by," Abdullah responded.

Fatina was intrigued, "What is it?"

"*Habiba.*" Abdullah articulated the name in a way that made Fatina feel like it was the first time she'd heard it. She liked it, even though it was a common name.

"Why Habiba? Who do you know with that name?" Fatina said with a hint of jealousy.

"You think there's someone out there that I want to name my daughter after? No, not at all. It's who she will be to me—to us. Every time I call her name, she'll know I love her."

Fatina's face beamed with joy, and she sensed how much her husband wanted to have a baby. "Ok, Abood. I never thought I'd give in so easily on our baby girl's name, but you win. It's a sweet name, just like you."

Fatina jumped on her feet and wrapped her arms tightly around Abdullah's neck. The conversation ended when Fatina finally agreed that they should visit a doctor.

FORGIVENESS

In rain, in cold, in summer, and under the falling autumn leaves is where all memories reside. The memories we cherish so are a mirage—deceiving and futile. I reach out to retain them, and as I put my hand out to grab ahold of them, the echoing laughter of the mirage sends a chill down my spine.
—Fatina

During adolescence, girls have one ultimate goal that will lead them to the epitome of happiness: finding love. Fatina was never opposed to the idea, but in addition to this instinctive passion, she had other goals in mind. The idea of finding her "Prince Charming" enthralled her young mind, but she also wanted to *become* something. She wanted to accomplish something in life other than having a family.

When Abdullah and Fatina got married, she realized how much their relationship had opened her eyes to so many hidden facets of life—things she couldn't have learned any other way.

"Abood," Fatina said. "I want to ask you something. I've mulled this over in my head so much, but to no avail. I need your superior knowledge and wisdom, my love." It was after one of their horseback-riding lessons, and Fatina and Abdullah sat on the beach alone. The evening breeze gently brushed Fatina's face; but when it enveloped her, she wrapped her arms around her legs and drew them close to her chest.

Sugar stood still, although her blonde mane fluttered lightly. This peaceful motion reminded Fatina of how nature gives them things that no oppressor could ever take away. She held on to the reins with one hand while she contemplated the horse. "I can't get enough of looking at her. She's such a beauty. *Mashallah*."

Abdullah adored the animal just as much and often spoke of her unmatched, God-given beauty. "You can talk to her. I do. She's a sensitive girl." Abdullah stood up, dusted off the back of his jeans, and put on his lightweight jacket before he sat back down beside Fatina. But when he saw her fold her arms and hug herself, as if she were cold, he took it right back off and put it over her shoulders.

"No, you keep it. You're wearing short sleeves." Fatina

said, brushing away the jacket. But Abdullah put it around her shoulders anyway.

"I can endure cold, rain, heat, and thunder for you, my baby," Abdullah said, stealing a kiss from Fatina's lips. "What's troubling you, sweetie? What did you want to ask me?"

Fatina let go of Sugar and tugged on Abdullah's arm. She was trying to see if it was OK to ask the question she was preparing to ask. Fatina's voice was low, "I just wonder sometimes if our lives would be different if you weren't part of the Resistance."

Abdullah understood his wife's fear, which had become evident after the horrific events they had gone through. At the beginning of their life together, Fatina showed strength and control. But months later, after she had faced trials, her vulnerability had been exposed. Abdullah knew only he could teach her to conquer her fears. For as far back as he could remember, his mother and the women in his neighborhood were strong and resilient. They weren't afraid to face the soldiers who barged into their homes to take away their sons. He still remembered how his mother had run after the soldier who dragged her son, Abdullah's brother, down the street and threw him in the back of a jeep. He hadn't been given time to change or even put on shoes. Um Abdullah ran down the street and threw her slippers in the vehicle for her son to wear.

But Fatina was nothing like his mother. He'd thought that all Palestinian women were inherently bold and powerful, but that wasn't the case with Fatina—especially after she'd been injured and continued to suffer aftershocks from the bombing.

Abdullah wanted to keep the conversation as lighthearted as possible, so he tried to appease her worries. "I've asked myself that exact same question, Lulu."

Fatina's face lit up and her eyes glimmered, "Same thoughts! And what did your mind tell you?" she asked.

Abdullah leaned back as Fatina clung to his arm. She had argued with him before about spending nights away from her and not being there when she needed him. During one of her frantic bouts of anger, she told him that she would never trust him again. At that moment, Abdullah had been in utter shock over the state of his wife and left the house immediately.

Abdullah knew that she wasn't in her right mind when she spewed such insults. He was hurt, but he would always have a soft spot for Fatina. Despite Fatina's harsh words, Abdullah was the person who she cherished and sought out whenever her own thoughts betrayed her. She loved his calm, matter-of-fact way of dealing with the toughest challenges. Whereas a problem might seem an overwhelming enigma to her, Abdullah would deal with it so easily.

"My grandfather told me so many stories when I was a kid, up until the day he died. There was one particular story that I never grew tired of hearing. I would always ask him to repeat it. It was about the day when Zionist gangs raided a nearby village, and the people of Al-Majdal fled to Gaza in terror. My grandpa brought all the documents relating to his property. After news circulated about Israelis murdering Palestinians in nearby villages, my grandpa fled his house there. He locked the front door and put the key in the sack he carried.

My grandfather's stories molded me. He'd always say at the end of every story, 'You, Abdullah … you and your brothers and your friends have the duty to bring back our land.' When I asked him how we could do that, he'd say, 'When you grow up, you'll figure it out.'

He often said that the only thing that could ever truly make him happy again would be to put the key back in the door of his home in Al-Majdal and open it."

Abdullah fell silent as if it hurt to recount those memories. Fatina listened attentively and sensed the sadness lingering over her husband's face. "Are you OK, Abood?"

"Yeah, but I just realized how much I still miss him after all these years. He died without fulfilling his dream, you know. I want to make his dream come true."

Abdullah's sorrow seemed to transfer to Fatina by the way she held on to him and caressed his arm. "Abood, how can you be so sure you will make your grandpa's dream come true? I don't see any sign of that happening soon. I only see more death and destruction."

Abdullah picked up Fatina's scarred hand and rubbed it gently. It was a habit he was fond of, especially after her injury. "You're right about one thing, habibti. We may not live to see our land liberated. But maybe our children will. It's not only about this being our goal; what matters is our being part of the liberation process."

Fatina sighed. She wanted to agree with her husband's idealistic concepts. "I know it's an honorable duty, and I can't argue with that. But, Abood, I daydream sometimes about living an ordinary life without so much adventure. I think about living a calm and peaceful life like people elsewhere. I dream of waking up on an island somewhere with nothing but the sounds of the palm trees swaying in the wind and the birds, and … Oh, just call me a dreamer."

Fatina's dark eyes always intrigued Abdullah. He never grew tired of gazing into them. "I would give anything to keep seeing that smile on your face and the magic in your eyes. Please don't lose it again. It keeps me alive," Abdullah pleaded. "I understand your fears, but here's something to think about to placate your troubled soul. Are people who don't work in the Resistance immune to death?"

Fatina replied instantly, "Nobody is immune to death."

"That's my point, sweetheart. Why should I live in fear of doing something I love when it may not be the cause of my death? Nobody knows how or when their time will come. So just try to make yourself content with our shared blessings and we'll be fine. Deal?"

Fatina was speechless. A tear escaped down her cheek. Abdullah's words struck her deep down. He was right, but right in a painful way. "Your words are the hard facts. I'll try to make them sink in."

After the long weeks of desertion and turbulence, Fatina owed her husband more than she had given him. "Abood. I'm—" Fatina's voice broke, and a gush of emotion shook her. A mixture of guilt, sorrow, and pity overcame her, but she needed to say it, "I'm sorry for all the stupid things I've said and done lately."

"Shh … It's all right. You're strong now. Never forget that, OK?" Abdullah whispered as he engulfed Fatina in his arms. It was where she felt safe. It was all she needed.

HAMZA

*Love can be found in the most common places,
like in the eyes of someone we meet by chance, in
someone no one else but you would notice with
your heart. At times, well-organized plans ruin
the essence of the moment. Sometimes, the best
moments of our lives are those that Allah sends
our way unexpectedly.*
—Hamza

Among the more prolific couples in Fatina's family were
her brother Hamza and his wife, Ayah. They had been
married only a year, but they already had one child—a
boy—born before they had even celebrated their first
wedding anniversary.

Like Abdullah, Hamza grew up with the Resistance.
The year his father had been shot by an Israeli soldier
and had to have his leg amputated was a turning point

in Hamza's life. His family watched as Hamza transformed from a good-looking, innocent teenager into the bulky, headstrong man whose very presence could fill a room.

Hamza's strong features didn't tarnish his attractiveness, they augmented it. Any girl would've considered him a catch. His role as a freedom fighter toughened him up and transformed him into a formidable character. But deep down, he was a romantic at heart. However, his family rarely saw that side of him—until he fell in love with Ayah. She was a widow and a few years older than he was, and in Palestinian culture, it is rare for a man to get involved with an older woman, particularly one that had been married before. Maybe that's why the news of his falling in love with Ayah came down on his family like a thunderbolt.

"Hamza, are you out of your mind, my son?" exclaimed Um Hamza the evening when her son disclosed his plans to marry Ayah.

"No, Mother. I know what I'm doing, and I know what I want and why," he replied, nonchalantly at first. Um Hamza's diminutive figure and placid demeanor were of no help to her when faced with Hamza's "outlandish thoughts" as she described them.

Hamza had known Ayah's late husband, Riyad. They were both in the same regiment. A spy for the Israelis was keeping tabs on Riyad and trying to link him to a number of Resistance operations. One day, in broad daylight, a dozen undercover Israeli soldiers surrounded Riyad in an ambush on one of the main roads in Gaza. Realizing that his end was approaching, Riyad chose to fight until his last breath.

Hamza met Ayah by chance at a bakery. She was carrying a bag of bread in one hand while holding her eighteen-month-old son Amir's hand in the other. Hamza recognized the boy, and an inadvertent look passed between Hamza and Ayah. It was a moment of destiny that transcended time and place.

At first, neither of them spoke, except with their eyes. Hamza read a lot in her eyes during those fleeting seconds. Her eyes reflected melancholy, despair, and shame for her circumstances. Hamza sensed this in the way Ayah's thin fingers trembled as she handed the cashier the money and fumbled to collect the change. Hamza's gaze embarrassed and confused Ayah.

Ayah was just beginning an attempt to return to life without her martyred husband. When she thought of how she had to go on without him, she felt paralyzed.

"Mother, please listen. Why do you and all the women in this place view women like Ayah as second-hand options ... as damaged goods? Ayah was married to the most honorable man and a dear friend. And now that he's been killed by those bastards from the Israeli occupation, why should she have to suffer for the rest of her life?" Hamza exhaled in exasperation.

Um Hamza's tiny figure seemed to shrink as her son grew more adamant in his pursuit of what he wanted. "She's a good woman," retorted Um Hamaza, "and one day, someone will marry her and—"

Hamza abruptly cut off his mother mid-sentence. "And that man will be me. Yumma listen, I saw her. She's a few years older than me, but she's young and … her beauty is mesmerizing. She's worthy of being loved in a way that only I can. I won't give up on her." Hamza was blushing, unsure how he'd just poured out his heart to his mother like that. Um Hamza threw up her hands in frustration and left the room.

"Big brother, I have to admit that I never expected this from you. It's an uncontested fact that you're all rough on the outside, but deep down, you're a hopeless romantic," Fatina said with a laugh.

Later that evening, Samira rebuked Fatina for supporting Hamza. "I thought you would knock some sense into your brother instead of encouraging his foolishness," she said bitterly, as Hamza stood pleased with his sister.

In terms of material things, Hamza didn't have much to offer Ayah. In the daytime, he worked occasionally as a teacher, but he was content with what Allah had given him. Growing up in the impoverished camp, he never thought his family's poverty was a barrier to anything—certainly not a barrier to love.

LOVERS UNITED

*Love knows no age or borders. I realized this
when I married Hamza only two weeks after we
got engaged. He insisted on rushing the wedding.
'I want you home with me,' he said. In Hamza,
I found the man who compensated for not only
my loss but my son's as well.*
—Ayah

"What are you staring at, sweetie?" Hamza whispered as he stood behind Ayah with his arms around her waist.

Ayah tingled at Hamza's touch and turned around to lay her head against his chest. She didn't want to answer his question. "I was looking at the stars and thinking about how they keep shining. No matter what happens, they just keep shining."

Hamza sensed that his wife might still be in an emotional transition period. "Are you happy with me?" he asked.

Ayah's hot tears fell on his chest as she pressed herself against him. "Yes, of course," she answered through muffled sobs.

"I don't know about you, but I'm happy," Hamza said, holding her tighter and trying to lift her mood. "I told my entire family that I was in love with the most beautiful woman on Earth, and no one could stop me from marrying her. I got what I wanted."

Ayah was confident of Hamza's sincere love. She cherished him and told him that he was a gift from God. "You're the best thing that ever happened to me. I just think about little Amir who will never see his father. It kills me when I think of it. But then I think of the thousands of other kids like him here and what each one must go through. At least Amir is in good hands with you."

Hamza stroked Ayah's hair, gently inhaling its fragrance as he pressed his chin against the top of her head. "When he grows up, he will be proud of who his father was. I promise to be like a father to him. I mean it. Do you doubt that?"

"No, I don't. I've only known you for a short time, but I trust you with all my heart. Amir already loves calling you Daddy."

Hamza felt that his marriage was unlike those of other men. He was privileged in so many ways. Ayah's calm beauty gave him peace and fulfillment, but it was more than just her physical appearance. Deep down, Hamza felt gratification and satisfaction when he saw her smile. Sometimes, he would hear her laughing as he entered the house, and he would realize how lucky he was to bring her out of her misery and loss.

Riyad had been his comrade, but Hamza felt awkward mentioning him in front of Ayah. Sometimes, he wanted to tell her about their adventures in the Resistance, and he would embark on a story, then cut it short. Ayah was even more uncomfortable commenting on any stories. She had mixed feelings about speaking her late husband's name. She contented herself with raising Riyad's only son and was devoted to loving Hamza with every fiber of her being.

THE WRITER

Contrary to popular beliefs freedom fighters are sensitive people. I know my role in serving my country well, but I also refuse to let that suppress my other passions. In many ways, no matter how polarized they may seem to others, all my passions intermingle to make me who I am.
—Abdullah

In addition to his involvement in the Resistance, Abdullah was a columnist at a local newspaper as well as some foreign magazines. He began as a fledging writer in college, but before he knew it, he found himself totally engrossed in the act of the written word. Many of his comrades thought the two jobs were at odds, but Abdullah vowed to prove them wrong.

One evening, after a long day of intensive training under severe conditions, the commanding officer finally had mercy on them and called an end to the day. Abdullah and his five comrades sat at the military training site. Despite their exhaustion, they still took pleasure in having conversations about their lives. Mahmoud, the most talkative, began, "All right, Abdullah, we've got you cornered. There's no escape."

Abdullah was lying on the grass with his hands behind his head. He didn't move, "OK, you've got me. But I'm warning you, man. I am not answering any questions about my love life. I've already given you all the details you need to know." Abdullah's warning drew *oohs* and *aahs* from the men who started to joke.

"Abood, you shouldn't keep your superior knowledge from us, or Allah will punish you. You know we're still young and immature, and we could use every bit of advice," one of them said as the others burst into laughter.

Mahmoud reasserted his authority over the scene. "Shut up, you guys. I'm serious. I want to ask Abdullah about his job. Abood, how can you be a fighter and a writer at the same time? We don't really understand it. These two things seem like polar opposites."

If there was one thing Abdullah loved, it was discussing his passion for writing. He sat up, stretched out his legs, and leaned back on his arms. His jade-green eyes matched the color of his military uniform, symbolizing the harmony between himself and his role as a freedom fighter.

Abdullah pointed to an old oak tree off in the distance. "How old do you think that tree is?"

Mahmoud glanced at the tree then back at Abdullah, "Over a hundred years old, I'd say. Is this a riddle or one of your romantic moments?"

The other men chuckled and one teased, "His romantic side is too much for us to take."

Still staring at the tree, Abdullah explained, "You see, I can write a whole story about that timeless tree—from its beginning to its end. Mahmoud, someone like you might think I'm just describing nature. But, if you read it with an open mind and heart, you'll see that I'm relating the history of Palestine and the great people like you who are building the best parts of our story."

All five pairs of eyes stared in astonishment at their comrade: the writer and Resistance fighter.

THE DIARY

June 2004
I discovered the many facets of beauty by delving
more into Abdullah's life. He's taught me many
things, but sometimes I've had to discover things
my own way, without feeling bad about intruding
upon his privacy. After all, we're one now, and
there should be no secrets between us.
—Fatina

Despite its worn-out and scratched surface, Abdullah's old wooden desk was his favorite piece of furniture in the apartment. Sometimes, Fatina would sit there to work on her assignments, but most of the time she preferred the small kitchen table. Once, when she taunted Abdullah about replacing the "old and collapsing" desk, he told her to be nice because all his best stories were written there.

Sitting at the desk on a warm summer day, Fatina pondered the neatly kept files Abdullah had on the far-right side. One was labeled "for publishing." A mid-sized blue notebook underneath it caught her eye. As Fatina leafed through it, she saw that the first page was titled "Me." Her curiosity was piqued. Without a second thought, she turned to the next page, which was titled "My Love."

"I don't believe any words in the dictionary could ever do you justice, my love, for I have discovered that you only speak one very special kind of language. I've been trying to learn that language to the best of my human efforts, but I'm still far behind.

When I was a child, my parents taught me that your soil was sacred. I don't remember my grandfather's face, but something he used to say still echoes in my ears: 'This land is thirsty, and that thirst can only be quenched with the blood of martyrs.'

Is it true, my love, that roses bloom from their blood? My grandfather died so long ago without seeing any roses. Will I also die with that wish in my heart?"

The piece was dated February 2004, just after midnight. Fatina's heart was racing; her mind was on fire. She had never read anything like that before. In fact, she never liked stories of martyrs because they gave her an eerie, haunting feeling. Even so, she continued to read. The next page was titled "My Angel."

"She flutters about like a delicate butterfly, so colorful, light, and full of life. In a garden filled with the most vivid and enchanting butterflies, she is beyond compare. Sometimes, I love to stand and watch her from a distance with her graceful movements. Although most of the time, she can't help but bring out the child within her, I still admire her every move. Her beauty is perceptible, yet the subliminal beauty she possesses is something only I can see. Even when she's sad or irritated, she never purses her lips. Her features stay intact, except for the turmoil in her lavish eyes, which I can instantly detect. Her beauty doesn't cause any commotion, it just heals. She's my only lover—Fatina."

As she finished reading, Fatina held the notebook close to her chest. She sensed how much pain Abdullah holds in his heart, yet it never stopped him from loving. She'd heard people say that those who are deprived of something fail to give it to others. But now she thought how absurd that saying was. Abdullah and many like him have suffered—and continue to suffer under the occupation—but that hasn't made them heartless or harsh. Abdullah was the embodiment of love and mercy.

OPERATION PRICELESS PREY

We had to learn everything our own way. In the
eyes of the world, our cause was at a standstill.
The 7,000-plus Palestinian prisoners in Israeli
jails were mere numbers to them. Yet, how
hypocritical and unfair that the opposite wasn't
true. No sympathy or even acknowledgment
whatsoever for our prisoners.
—Abdullah

The operation was to begin at eleven o'clock at night.
Abdullah was in charge of nine members of the Elite
Regiment who would carry out what was called
"Operation Priceless Prey."

Since morning, Abdullah had been checking and
rechecking the details of the plan. Four members

were to climb through the tunnel leading to an Israeli military base and wait at the other end. The remaining five were to be stationed above ground at a different opening. Days and weeks of monitoring had given the team a close-up view of the number of Israeli soldiers who patrolled the border and when they changed shifts.

The five who were to come face-to-face with the enemy would use silencers to eliminate the squad, save for one, whom they would capture and deliver safely to the four freedom fighters waiting in the tunnel. This prisoner would become the most priceless prisoner who could later be offered in exchange for many more incarcerated Palestinian prisoners.

From the long days and nights closely observing the Israeli soldiers, Abdullah and his team had noticed that the closest military vehicle was stationed at least nine miles (fifteen kilometers) away from the squad—too far away to be of any real help to them.

Peering through his binoculars, Abdullah observed the youthful Israeli soldiers lounging by their vehicles and flirting with their female comrades. Abdullah reflected on the disparity between their sense of duty and his. He served a worthy cause, loyal to his people and ready to die in defense of the land he loved. The Israeli soldiers didn't care. Their only concern was staying alive until their time of discharge.

Abdullah stood holding his chart and called out code names, "Jaguar, Thunder, Fury, Lightning." He took a deep breath and paused before announcing the next name. With a catch in his voice, he said, "Legend I." For an instant, he gazed into a pair of eyes he knew all too well.

Despite the masked face, Omar's fierce, sharp eyes pierced Abdullah's steadfast composure. Life, in that instant, hung between them like the last grains in an hourglass, quickly slipping away.

Abdullah labored to keep his facial features hardened. He clenched his teeth and fists, laboring mightily not to betray the emotions welling up within him. If only he could lift the mask off Omar's face and see what lay hidden deep behind those unflinching eyes.

Abdullah's chest began to heave, unable to hold back any longer. With his pounding heart about to break, Abdullah finally quavered: "What purpose can words serve us now, my friend?"

Abdullah was depleted. Omar held out his arm, clasped Abdullah's hand and squeezed it tightly as if he had rehearsed that dreadful moment. "Till we meet in Heaven, Abdullah."

Omar quickly loosened his grip on Abdullah's hand, and Abdullah knew that his friend was slipping away from him. He regained his composure and patted his dear friend on the back as he shouted at the top of his lungs, "Go, Legend I! May Allah be with you always!" He continued as Omar headed toward the tunnel, "Legend I, show Allah your best!"

Those still waiting to hear their names called were staring at Abdullah. He was their commanding officer, but before their eyes, they saw him strip himself of the stern disguise he'd worn. He tried hard to come off as a ferocious and fearless lion, but his love—his humanity—surfaced at that critical moment, and he felt naked to their watchful eyes.

As Omar disappeared down the tunnel, Abdullah snapped back to reality and the intensity of the moment. Adrenaline gushed through his veins as he shouted the names of the remaining men. With lightning speed, they all vanished down the tunnel.

In a few moments that earthen shaft would, through their heroic exploits, soon gain renown and be named the "Tunnel of Freedom."

The operation did not take as long as planned. The group whose mission was above ground accomplished their task seamlessly in record time.

Abdullah, monitoring his men during those seemingly endless twenty-five minutes, heard gunshots. Then he heard an uproarious *"Allahu Akbar!"* A chill ran down Abdullah's spine as he recognized Omar's voice. But he couldn't help but wonder: *Do I pray that he comes back safely or that he goes to Hasna? How can I wish death upon him? He's my best friend.*

Abdullah inhaled and exhaled deeply, murmuring to himself, *"Ya Allah Ya Allah."* He tried to speak louder to give himself power. But then suddenly, four men emerged from the tunnel carrying a body. The operation was going as planned.

When they were planning the mission, the only part of the operation that was going to be challenging was retrieving the bodies of any freedom fighters killed. It was no secret that Israeli soldiers withheld the bodies of Palestinian martyrs to steal their organs and then buried them in mass graves. Abdullah would not allow this to happen to Legend I. His body would be returned home for a massive military procession.

FEUD

This is another test of time that's very hard to pass. Even if we do get through it, there will still be traces left deep down to resurface at every new struggle. I tried to make Abood see that together we could make it through anything.
—Fatina

Fatina was furious. A battle was raging inside her, and Abdullah's long silence further fueled the flame. After Omar's martyrdom, Abdullah's weight loss was palpable. His face became gaunt, his cheekbones angular. He still maintained his strong build, but his waistline grew smaller.

Fatina tried to contain herself and not allow anger to consume her. But Abdullah's eerie silence suffocated the life out of her. He refused to talk about anything.

Admittedly, she wasn't a trained therapist, but she knew that if they talked about it, he might feel better. Instead, he shut her out, neutralizing her attempts to break the cycle of isolation and depression.

She confronted him once about suffering from grief, and Abdullah lashed back at her: "I may seem abnormal to you. But ask anyone, and they'll tell you I'm fine."

Fatina's cheeks grew hot from the anger boiling inside her, and her heart began to palpitate. "You're completely devoid of humanity if you think that Omar's death hasn't affected you, and you know it. Of course—you think I'm the only one who has dealt with depression and madness! You seem to think that you're impenetrable when you know very well that's all an act. Maybe if you would stop acting—"

Abdullah struggled to suppress his anger. He folded his arms across his chest and turned his back to her. She had never talked to him this way before, but she was fed up and she wanted him to know it.

Abdullah stormed out of the apartment and slammed the door behind him, leaving Fatina fuming.

Some time passed before she could figure out what to do with herself. She needed to take out all the negative energy on something, so she stomped her way to the kitchen. The sink was full of the day's dishes, cups, spoons, and other utensils that had piled up. She remembered a piece of foolish advice from the women in her family who said that washing dishes was relaxing. She certainly didn't agree with them, but, at that moment, she was desperately trying to find a way to calm down the fiery beast writhing inside her. Maybe the water would have a calming effect.

She turned on the faucet and held up a cup. She rubbed it with the sponge with such force that it fell from her hand and shattered. Her finger caught the sharp edge of the glass, "Damn it!" she roared.

It was a slight injury, but there was a lot of blood. She felt more anger than hurt. At the moment she screamed, the apartment door opened and closed.

This is not the best time for Abdullah to come home, she thought.

Fatina's yelp pierced Abdullah's ears as he shut the door. He ran into the kitchen, his eyes searching around to see what had happened. Fatina was holding a rag and pressing it against her finger.

Abdullah approached her slowly, saying, "What happened?"

She jerked her hand away and retorted, "Nothing. I'm fine." Her facial features spoke more of restlessness than pain. But Fatina was still not herself. She didn't want this to be an excuse for him to make her forget the root of their problem.

She walked toward the window and pushed it open. Maybe the air would cool down her temper. Why was she being so mean? She wanted Abdullah to talk to her, to share his suffering with her, to acknowledge her role in his life like she viewed his presence in hers. But he always wanted to assume the role of the staunch commander who had everything under control. She wasn't going to allow it this time.

"Just go away," she whimpered. "You take care of yourself, and I'll take care of myself."

Abdullah had left earlier to avoid a battle, but now he could see that a confrontation was inevitable. "Fatina, stop it! You know I've been through this before, and I'll be okay, and—"

"Of course. I'm sure you have lots of good friends that you can talk to," Fatina blurted out with rage. "But why do you treat me like an ignorant child? Just because you're in the Resistance doesn't mean that you have to act like you have a heart of stone."

Abdullah gazed at her, his eyes shifting down to her finger, which was now dripping blood onto her clothes. She was shaking and distraught. "Your finger is still bleeding," Abdullah said, holding out his hand to press her finger against his shirt.

Even though Abdullah was being sweet and trying to take care of her, Fatina found the only way to vent her anger was to lash out. She hated the feeling of defeat. Without thinking, she slapped him across the face with all her might.

Abdullah didn't budge. He just kept pressing her finger against his shirt. Feeling as if his eyes were piercing her very soul, Fatina broke down and sobbed against his half-buttoned shirt.

"I'm sorry," Abdullah whispered as he held Fatina tightly. "You may think I don't acknowledge your presence in my life, but I do it in my own way. I may not be talkative, but it's difficult for me to communicate after the death of a loved one. And you can be sure that I haven't been talking to anyone else. If I feel the need to talk, I'll come to you and … we can go to our rock."

The stars continued to shine over Abdullah's world, but with Omar gone, he lost the harmony. He sat on the floor of the balcony that night with Fatina next to him. She was holding her bandaged finger slightly elevated. Abdullah's tone was flat and sad as he said, "I know that these are the same stars that Omar and I used to sit under, but they seem so different now. They radiate sadness and fill me with a hollow feeling."

Guilt started to gnaw at Fatina as he finally began to communicate with her. She was confused about whether she should apologize to Abdullah or proceed with this long-awaited conversation.

She gazed at the stars and tried to find the attraction that hypnotized Omar and Abdullah. The stars were glimmering above, giving light and beauty to all humankind, but only some could savor that beauty.

"I've never stargazed myself or understood this world above, but you showed me," Fatina began. "The stars haven't changed. It's you that's changed, Abood. You no longer see them with an open heart—in a way that lets you take in their beauty. I think it's only a matter of time before you return to your old self." She wondered if her words made any sense to him.

"But you see, Lulu, I can never be my *old* self. I'm a different person now. We can't go back in time and be who we were a month ago or even a week ago. We keep evolving in new ways. What we go through changes us forever—maybe it's for the better, maybe it's not. But one thing is for sure: it does change us. The beauty is there, but the spark in my heart has diminished." Abdullah sighed as if to relieve his chest from a heavy burden.

"Abood, you told me once that people can change to become better people or bad ones. Are you saying you've regressed?"

"It's not that black or white. It's a constant battle that I have to keep fighting. I've lost too many good people in my life. Sometimes, this makes life seem so trivial. Sometimes, I wish life were a person, so I could spit on it and push it off a cliff. At other times, I keep remembering my grandfather's words, and I muster the energy to stay strong. Either way, it's a struggle."

As Fatina thought about Abdullah's words, she turned her head slightly toward him then she returned to gazing at the sky.

THE LEGACY

*When loved ones depart this earthly plane,
we feel a duty to keep them alive somehow.
Sometimes, we do things that they used to do
because we know they're watching over us and
we want to make them smile down at us. I've
begun to question whether time really heals
all wounds. I know time goes on, but can the
deep-seated scars ever be healed?*
—Abdullah

After Omar's death, Abdullah constantly thought about who Omar was and what he stood for. Moments of pensive meditation rewarded him with striking revelations. He thought about Omar's unmatched kindness and love toward others, and he thought about all the sacrifices he had made.

With Omar gone, Abdullah felt an enormous void in his soul. He hadn't realized how much Omar's absence would haunt him every day. Abdullah frequently had conversations inside his head: *I must be strong for the sake of my other comrades. They need me in the same way I needed Omar.* If he wanted Omar to stay alive inside him, he would have to carry his legacy. His comrades needed support. Their military duties seemed to suck the life out of them at times.

Abdullah constantly prayed to Allah for strength: *Please Allah, give me the power to go on. I know that without your divine care, I will be lost. I am weak without you, my lord. All strength is from you only. Please make me strong.*

In those moments of prayer, Abdullah was himself. He made no attempts to hide his feeling of helplessness. In fact, he knew that his sincerest prayers were those in which he admitted his need for Allah's guidance and mercy. Those prayers soothed his aching heart, and he believed they would be answered.

From where he sat under the old oak tree at the training site, Abdullah glanced sideways. His comrades were sitting nearby, about to have lunch. He knew that, as usual, it would probably be chicken and rice that they picked up from a local restaurant.

At such moments, Abdullah saw his comrades in their most genuine form—human and spontaneous.

They joked with each other and hardly talked about politics or the Resistance, feeling free just to be themselves without fear of rebuke.

A sudden burst of shrill laughter resounded from the group, so Abdullah got up to see what was happening. He walked toward them and said, "Hey, what did I miss?"

The men were still laughing and one of them, Ali, responded through his cackle, "Not until you tell us what sort of treasure you found under that tree."

Abdullah sat down to eat with them, and to his surprise, this time it was homemade chicken and rice. His face lit up as he said, "That looks good!"

"Indeed! Food made with love."

"Yeah, at least we won't find any cockroaches like we did—" Ali started to say before Abdullah abruptly cut him off.

"Shut up! Or I swear I'll smash this tray against your face," Abdullah snapped. "You guys are making me sick to my stomach with such talk."

"Chill, man," responded Ali. "This is my mom's cooking. Please respect that."

"I'm sorry. It's just that Omar used to love this dish," Abdullah reminisced aloud. "You guys remember that?"

They had already immersed themselves in the food and weren't about to let Abdullah's mournful memories ruin their meal. "But his horeeyah is probably feeding him lots of heavenly fruit now."

"Yeah. I can picture them now," Ali remarked through his bites and spoonfuls.

But again, Abdullah intervened, "Hey, please keep those images in your head."

"Ya Allah! You can't stop disciplining us, can you Abdullah?" Ali countered.

"I can't help it!" Abdullah confessed. "Besides, if I let your imagination run wild, we'll probably end up in an intimate movie scene."

Ali's mood suddenly changed, as if he'd only been putting on a show to make the others laugh. "Yeah, Omar always blushed at this kind of talk. *Allah yir-hamu* … I miss him."

FAREWELL

*I've always dreaded goodbyes. They leave me with
an empty hollow feeling that is hard to overcome.
I can fight in a war zone, but bidding a loved one
farewell has always been my weakness.*
—Abdullah

*On that day, my faithful friend, when I saw you for the
last time, I felt something different and inexplicable. You
lay there lifeless in your military uniform and blood was
still trickling from your forehead. I touched it lightly, care-
ful not to disturb your eternal sleep.*

*The crimson red drops had an unmistakable fragrance
unlike any I'd ever smelled before. If Fatina's perfume has
the effect of awakening my senses, the scent of your precious
blood filled my heart with melancholy. Was it the smell of
Heaven? Will I ever know?*

The smile so magically displayed on your serene face puzzled me all the more. I wanted to hold your shoulders and shake you. I wanted to implore you to tell me what had been revealed to you. But your divine presence silenced me. I could only bring myself to bury my head in your chest and cry. Your body was still warm, making it hard to believe that you were dead. I can't begin to explain the yearning that ravages my soul. Please visit me in my dreams.

I was always intrigued by how you could resist earthly temptations, but now I know that you had other matters on your mind. In your life, during our time together, you taught me so much.

In you, I found all the goodness that others lacked. After your death, more of you has been revealed to me. I see your face at every corner and under every tree I pass. Sometimes, I stop at a tree and just stare, as if by standing there long enough, I could somehow summon you to return. I've kept your bloodstained handkerchief, and not a day goes by when I don't sniff it to reassure myself that you are up there watching over me.

Fatina watched from the doorway as Abdullah put down his pen. He closed his notebook gently and pushed it aside. Fatina had continued to read his diary, and from the look on her husband's face, she guessed that he must have been writing about either Ahmed or Omar.

"Come in," Abdullah said to Fatina without looking. He covered his face with his hands as Fatina came to his side. Abdullah was always her rock—her source of strength and power. But sometimes, it was no use pretending and suppressing sadness. Fatina drew his head to her chest and stroked his hair, "It's OK, Abood. Just let it all out."

REBIRTH

So many episodes of sadness and grief had passed that I found it hard to comprehend that a new chapter was unfolding in my life. I never thought I would find the heart or stamina to heal, but God's all-encompassing grace penetrated our grieving hearts. Fatina and I had something to be happy about.
—Abdullah

Fatina stood at the window dressed in her abaya waiting for Abdullah to arrive. He'd called and told her to get ready. It was summer vacation, and, as usual, kids were playing soccer in the empty space next to the mosque. Fatina could see that the boys were barefoot, but it didn't keep them from playing. There were shrills of excitement mixed with laughs and boisterous shouts when a player scored a goal.

Fatina was visiting the gynecologist for some tests. A taxi stopped near the mosque, and it took Fatina only a quick glimpse to recognize the back of Abdullah's head as he got out of the cab. He jogged toward the boys holding up both hands in greeting. Abdullah was met with a collective cheer as he entered the field and kicked the ball at his feet.

Fatina remembered how she used to watch the World Cup with her brothers. She didn't understand soccer, but she and her friends debated over which player was the cutest. Each girl would choose one and fantasize about him. Fatina laughed at her teenage self, excited to be watching her own real-life hero—her husband—whose lithe figure moved with energy as he tackled the ball.

She cheered, "Go Abood!" as she watched him strike and kick the ball into the net. As a loud roar erupted from the boys, Abdullah raised his hand and bumped fists with the boys as he made his way off the field.

Fatina was apprehensive about the upcoming exam, especially since it was with a male doctor. Previously, the doctor had explained the tests he was going to perform and showed her the utensils and equipment he would use. At that time, Fatina panicked and refused to cooperate.

Days passed before Fatina could get herself to start the tests, but the ordeal went easier than she had imagined. The doctor's diagnosis showed that the couple had no physical problems that would keep them from conceiving.

Perhaps it was a coincidence or maybe a matter of choosing the right time to come into the world. Either way, an infant was conceived a month later. By then, Fatina and Abdullah had been married three years, so both families were overjoyed with the news. Her mother-in-law boasted that if the baby was a boy, he would surely be handsome like Abdullah, and if it was a girl, she'd definitely inherit all of Fatina's beauty. "I just hope the boy doesn't turn out to be stubborn like his father," Um Abdullah joked.

Fatina was a bit surprised by the remark. She never thought of Abdullah as stubborn. In fact, she felt she was the obstinate one, and Abdullah was always trying to placate her. "Was Abood stubborn when he was a kid, *khalto*?" Fatina asked.

Um Abdullah put her hand to her heart in a feigned gesture of exasperation, "He always had to have his way. I never thought he'd outgrow it. But he changed a lot after high school."

Fatina grinned as she tried to imagine Abdullah being stubborn and defiant, "I can't imagine how he must have been," she said.

"That's because he's a sweet and gentle man now. He changed considerably after he married you."

Um Abdullah had just finished talking when Abdullah came in. "I thought I heard someone say my name."

"Yes indeed, my son. I was telling your wife what you were like before you married her."

Abdullah walked over and kissed his mother's forehead, then he sat beside Fatina and wrapped an arm around her shoulder. "No matter what you say about me, she's stuck with me forever," he said with a laugh as he kissed his wife on the cheek.

At the beginning of their marriage, Fatina wasn't passionate about having children. But she had changed her mind. Now, she understood how precious it was to have this baby inside her. "It feels strange to have part of you growing inside me, Abood," she said as she leaned her head against his shoulder.

"It's part of both of us," Abdullah said as he stroked Fatina's cheek.

Um Abdullah had gone into the kitchen to finish preparing dinner. She was positively elated, and in celebration, she was making her special homemade *maftoul*. When she returned to the living room, she announced that dinner was ready. She watched her son and his wife sitting dreamily, as if they were in a different world. "You two come eat, and then you can go back to your dream world." She was jabbering excessively from happiness. This baby was going to be the most precious blessing in the world to her.

On May 12, 2007, Fatina went into labor while Abdullah was away. He had always assured her that he would be right by her side to witness the birth of their first child, but he knew that he couldn't guarantee that. His variable schedule of night and morning shifts made it impossible for him to know if he could be there to hold her hand and hear their baby's first scream of life. Yet he would always say to her, "*Inshallah habibti*, I'll do all I can to be there for you."

That day as the sun was just beginning to creep above the horizon, Fatina began having contractions. She was still a week away from her due date, but her mother and mother-in-law had given her enough information to know that she was going into labor. It was unlike any kind of pain she had ever experienced. She cried out Abdullah's name as she was rushed to the hospital in their neighbor's car.

At the hospital, Um Abdullah quieted Fatina and told her she would send her other son to find Abdullah. Fatina was perspiring. The nurse was giving her directions to inhale and exhale whenever she felt a contraction.

She lay there for two hours with little sign of any prog-ress. Writhing with the pain and pressure of every contraction, she pushed with all her strength, but the baby wasn't moving. As the contractions increased in intensity and frequency, Fatina became utterly exhausted. Although she tried to think about the beauty and joy of bringing a new life into the world, she couldn't help but focus on the horrendous pain she was experiencing. She tried to concentrate on the fact that women kept having babies despite going through the excruciating pain she was enduring.

After another two hours had passed, Fatina felt completely drained of all her strength. She began crying as pain and fear and a feeling of helplessness consumed her. Then suddenly, she felt a hand holding hers—Abdullah had arrived. She didn't see his face, but she held his hand. This physical bond between them seemed to radiate energy and strength from his body to hers. Reinvigorated with this new energy, Fatina screamed and gave one more forceful push. Her chest heaved from the exertion. Before her breathing was back to normal, she heard the tiny but piercing cry of her baby. It was the sweetest sound she'd ever heard, but her body was fatigued, and she quickly fell into a deep sleep.

HABIBA

Is this the moment every woman on Earth anxiously awaits? A bundle of tiny beadlike eyes and soft miniature hands has been placed in my arms. No wonder I'm experiencing a new feeling I've never encountered before. It's pacifying and nurturing and indescribable in every way.
—Fatina

Fatina was drifting in and out of consciousness—that moment between sleeping and waking. A familiar scent filled her nostrils. It was a scent she knew all too well, but she couldn't manage to open her eyes.

Fatina could hear voices all around her. She recognized them but was still trying to come to. She felt someone softly squeezing and caressing her hand. That could only be one person. Fatina opened her eyes to meet Abdullah's. His glistening eyes radiated warm rays of love and contentment.

Fatina managed to drowsily articulate, "You're here." She attempted to reach out to him, but Abdullah leaned over and put his face against her head. She felt a rush of warm energy run through her veins as he whispered before kissing her forehead, "I promised I'd be here, remember?"

Habiba brought a new energy into Fatina's and Abdullah's home. By every means, she took over their minds and hearts. They would lie in bed with Habiba between them and contemplate her tiny parts. "Just think, Abood … this baby was inside me. It's hard to believe, isn't it?"

"Yeah. It's a miracle that takes place every minute around the world. Kind of makes me think how we're oblivious to this life cycle," Abdullah's voice trailed off in wonder.

"I bet you have something to write about now, don't you?" Fatina teased.

When Abdullah went to do his night duty for the Resistance, Fatina busied herself with Habiba. The baby had made her think of things in different ways. She missed Abdullah's presence, but she realized that, soon enough, their daughter would too. Her heart ached at the thought. She thought about the other children in the neighborhood whose fathers were in the Resistance and about those whose fathers had been killed.

She wanted Habiba to see her father every day for the rest of her life. She thought about Ayah's son Amir, who had no memory of his martyred father. It was true that Hamza treated him like his own son, but one day, when he was older, Amir would realize that he never really knew his own father.

These thoughts weighed heavily on Fatina. They practically smothered her and she found herself shaking her head sideways as if she could get rid of them that way.

She promised Abdullah she would be strong, but every day she faced new tests that she felt unable to tackle. She wanted to be strong like so many of the other women in her neighborhood, but instead, she felt powerless. All these chaotic thoughts were intruding upon her peace of mind, rendering her almost helpless.

She thought about how Abdullah's mother faced so many hardships with a triumphant spirit and grace. Fatina wished it was contagious—that she could do the same. Maybe it was. She thought of going downstairs to talk to her, but it was nearly midnight.

Suddenly, her thoughts were interrupted by a key turning in the apartment door. Abdullah's return made all those disturbing thoughts vanish from her mind—at least momentarily. It was the only thing that tethered her to reality. "Hey. I came back early," he said quietly, noticing that Habiba was asleep. "I missed her."

Fatina remembered how much her husband wanted to choose the name Habiba, which means "the loved one." She could see now that it was the perfect name. "So, you missed *her*? Your tune has certainly changed," Fatina tried to eye him sternly, but she couldn't suppress a grin.

Abdullah smiled with slight guilt, "Oh God, I know you won't let this one pass. I'll have to swear on the holy Quran that I missed *you* too." Then he tried to downplay the sarcasm in his voice, "But, you know, it's like whenever you get something new; you get really excited at first." Abdullah looked at Fatina to see if she would buy it.

She decided not to give him a hard time. Moments before, she was envisioning terrifying things, and now he was here. She was just happy to see him come home to her and Habiba. "You know, I'm a nice person," she said.

Abdullah wrapped his arms around her and squeezed her tight, "You're precious."

WISDOM

Bombings, displacement, and the absence of my husband: These were the trials I faced as a result of the Israeli occupation. They were events that would make or break me. I decided that I already had enough broken pieces inside me and would not allow any more.

—Fatina

Fatina was beginning to realize that the world she had once longed for was just a silly dream. There were moments that she cherished, yet they seemed so distant that they lost their effect.

One evening, Fatina and Abdullah decided to visit their rock at the beach. They left Habiba with Um Abdullah and set out to their sacred place.

"I once thought that all it took to be happy was to find love," she said to Abdullah. "But lately, I've begun to question everything. Once you get something that you've wanted so badly for so long, you discover that there's more to happiness than just that one thing." A series of events flashed before her, mostly grief and sadness.

Abdullah was taken aback by his wife's metamorphosis. Three years into their marriage, he was beginning to sense a rapid change in the way Fatina perceived things. If her heart told her she was right about something, nothing could change her mind. Nevertheless, she and Habiba were his source of joy and stability.

Fatina continued, "It seems that we are the only ones on Earth trapped in this hellhole known as Gaza. We're getting slaughtered. We have to stand up for ourselves and fight, but we get ostracized for doing so. Nobody cares about us. Our men have to stay out all night guarding our country, but they could die in the process. This is the world our parents grew up in, and it's the same one we grew up in. And now we pass it on to our children. It's a vicious cycle, Abood."

Abdullah was stunned into silence as his wife ended her sudden exposition of thoughts and feelings. He had never heard her sum up their situation so bluntly. It made his already aching heart even heavier. He wanted so badly to console his wife, but he knew that his ordinary sentence of assurance "It's going to be all right," would sound silly somehow. Instead he said, "You're right in every way, Lulu. I just want you to see that this is another piece of the big puzzle you're forming in your head. It's a very crucial piece, but there are still many other pieces to be found."

"Do you have any of those other pieces?" she asked, only half-joking.

"I may have a few," he replied. "See, whether we live here in this hellhole as you call it, or far away in a safe haven of wealth and prosperity, to me, it seems the same. Do you think I don't have similar thoughts of just running away from it all and going somewhere to start new lives and live happily ever after?"

"You're too smart to believe such nonsense, I'm sure." Fatina answered.

"So … you don't believe in happy endings?" Abdullah probed.

"It's embarrassing to even admit that I used to." Fatina was despondent. She wanted to believe that happy endings do exist.

The despair in Fatina's voice tugged at Abdullah's heart. He didn't want his wife to lose her spontaneity and zest for life and the child within her. These qualities were hard to maintain in their present situation, but Fatina tried to hang on to some of them.

What Abdullah said made sense. Fatina grasped the meaning behind it, but she still felt that despite all the harshness they had suffered—which was not likely to end anytime soon—she still wanted to embrace the good things in her life.

"If it was only you and me, Aboodi, we could dedicate our lives to ridding the world of evil, but we have a child now—a child who still hasn't experienced anything. I want her to see the beauty in life even if I have to struggle to find it for her. She doesn't have to know how ugly this world is. It would be cruel if she did. I want to protect her childhood in every way I can." Fatina was adamant and assured despite her sorrow.

Whenever Abdullah was unable to find the right words to comfort his wife, he'd just pull her close to him and it would momentarily wash away all her fears. Abdullah's love and warmth had a way of strengthening her and quelling her fears.

There was a long silence. Abdullah imagined Omar looking down on him urging him to hang in there and stay strong and persistent. Despite all the misery and injustice he and his people had experienced, Abdullah knew it would end someday. His faith in his people's cause always inspired him and lifted his spirits. There was also a tremendous sense of defiance forming inside him. He wasn't going to let other humans subjugate him or dictate how he lived. Whether or not his homeland was under occupation, he was born a free man and he would die a free man.

"Let's go home, Abood." Abdullah held her hand as she jumped off the rock, and they began walking back. The beach was only ten minutes from their home."

"We just need to trust in Allah and keep fighting," Abdullah attempted to explain. "We can't turn back now. If we do, we'll lose everything we've fought so hard for, and Omar and all the other martyred freedom fighters will have given their lives in vain. If we give up now, the world will still keep moving forward with all its good and bad. So we have to keep going and just embrace the journey. I'm not being philosophical Lulu.... It's just the way my mind shows me the world."

Fatina thought of young men living elsewhere and what kind of lives they had. She thought of how, despite their young age, Abdullah and his comrades had devoted their lives to their country.

When they got home, Habiba was asleep. Abdullah cuddled her in his arms, planted a soft kiss on her forehead, and carried her upstairs to their apartment. Fatina was still in her talkative mood.

"Abood, have you ever watched those Turkish soap operas?" Fatina asked.

Abdullah was getting drowsy, yet his curiosity prompted him to reply. "Hmmm, I don't think so, but I've heard my sisters talking about them. The hero is Kareem, and he's in love with a Fatima or a Noor, right?"

Fatina laughed. "Yes, but it doesn't matter. My point is that girls are obsessed with watching those soap operas. I watched a couple of episodes, but then I found you, so I stopped. But some girls think that in real life men will be just like those TV lovers."

"I'm intrigued," Abdullah replied sleepily. "I'm serious. I've always wondered how those shows manage to keep everyone glued to their TVs. I was starting to think I was missing out on something."

"Those actors are a farce, yet girls fail to notice people like you," Fatina said as she stroked Abdullah's forehead. "But you know what, Abood? You're the only hero in my eyes." Fatina laid her head on Abdullah's forehead and said, "I'm glad that I captured a real hero."

SURVIVAL

December 2008–November 2012
It was death from above. Families wiped out in
scores; midnight bombings of houses, military sites,
open land, factories, and government buildings.
It was a fiendish nightmare, but we survived.
There's something about surviving that makes you
feel triumphant.
—Abdullah

It was late December and life-changing horror was about to befall the people of Gaza. Habiba was a year and a half old. She'd recently started talking and had been walking since just before her first birthday. Since then, their apartment had never been the same.

Fatina was constantly chasing her around and snatching objects from her tiny grasp. Finally, Fatina gave up and decided to clear the way for her, putting away all the decorative figurines and anything that Habiba could smash. It was easier to just let her have her way around the house without chasing her all day.

Abdullah spoiled Habiba from the start. He even began coming home from work early just to see her. He was always bringing home something for her. He told Fatina that he found it hard to resist buying stuff for his little girl. "I'm officially jealous now, Abood," Fatina declared one day.

"I was waiting for you to say that, my love," Abdullah smiled and presented her with the red rose he was hiding behind his back. "This is only for you." He handed it to Fatina with a sweet, long kiss.

"I have to admit that you're trying to be fair," Fatina conceded.

That next day at noon, they were in the living room, Fatina with her laptop propped up on her lap, Abdullah sitting next to her playing with Habiba. The TV was on.

Suddenly, the TV screen went blank as the electricity cut out. When it came back on a few minutes later, Fatina found herself staring in horror at a picture of mutilated corpses.

Then they heard an explosion in the distance—not too close but not too far away, either. People began screaming in the streets. Fatina held her breath and listened for another explosion. It didn't take long before she heard a series of booms—both near and far—rocking the atmosphere. From the living room window, Fatina and Abdullah could see black smoke billowing through the air. Commotion filled the streets as people tried to find out where the smoke was coming from.

The TV screen showed that the corpses belonged to Palestinian police cadets. An earlier air strike had hit a graduation ceremony at a nearby police academy. Without knowing where the howling screams were coming from, Fatina began to wail as well.

When Habiba started crying, Abdullah ran to the TV and turned it off. He immediately knew that the Israelis had decided to go on a killing spree from above. He enveloped Fatina and Habiba in his arms. Fatina was shaking frantically, "Abood, what's happening....?" she panted between sobs.

The attack lasted for three weeks. During that time, bombs dropped from F-16s leveled buildings. Houses were shelled, and the crumbling rubble crushed those inside. The UNRWA schools where people took refuge were targeted with white phosphorous, which filled the air with smoke, burned the skin of innocent bystanders, and ignited buildings. It was more than a nightmare; it was a living hell.

Fatina and her family survived, but many of her relatives and people she knew were not so fortunate. One family in the neighborhood of Al-Najjar was completely wiped out when F-16s shelled their house. And Anwar, the cousin with whom Fatina had argued about the Resistance, was killed in a car bombing when a targeted missile hit the car in which he was riding. Ironically, he was killed by something he believed was only a danger to the freedom fighters.

After the attack on Gaza in 2008, Abdullah took a break from the Resistance for a while. His family had already been through enough hardship, and Fatina was in a fragile state. His presence was vitally needed at home.

However, when the Israelis launched more attacks in Gaza in November 2012, Abdullah returned to the front lines. By then, Habiba was six years old and was extremely attached to her father. Whenever she saw him don his military uniform, she would kiss him and tell him, "Go get the bad guys."

Abdullah wanted Habiba to be strong. He'd raised her to be someone who wasn't afraid of anything, real or imagined. He realized that it was his job to mold her, so he decided to make Habiba the strongest girl he possibly could.

Like most girls, Habiba was into dolls and nail polish. She loved to play with dolls with Fatina, but when Abdullah came home, she'd run to him and ask if he won any battles that day.

"Yes, honey," he'd say. "We won again."

"Did you catch any bad guys?" Habiba would ask.

"Oh, not today," Abdullah would respond playfully. "They all ran away."

Fatina listened to those playful conversations between Abdullah and Habiba. In a way, she was content for Habiba to grow into a powerful woman, but she wanted her to live like other girls around the world. Fatina realized that even if she could buy Habiba all the toys in the world, she could never buy her peace and security.

During Fatina's childhood, Gaza was occupied, and Israeli soldiers stood guard on the streets. Fatina would tug on her brother's hand when they passed by the soldiers. Hamza always told her that she was safe with him, but there was something about those heavily armed soldiers that would frighten any child.

Fatina thought about Abdullah's grandfather and how he died without seeing his dream of returning to his homeland come true. She wondered if it was going to be the same for her and her family. More than sixty years later, the situation still had not changed.

Fatina wanted her daughter to have an idyllic childhood: to be free like a butterfly without fear of being bombed, to dress up as a princess, to sleep soundly and have childish dreams, not nightmares that would cause her to wake up trembling in fear.

She decided to discuss this with Abdullah one night after he had put Habiba to sleep.

"Abood, I admire the way you're dealing with Habiba and raising her to be more like you," Fatina began, subtly acknowledging that she still wasn't the woman Abdullah hoped she would be.

Abdullah pulled Fatina close to him as he stretched his legs across the coffee table in the living room. "She's already like you. She's got those mysterious and daring eyes." Abdullah said as he brushed his lips against her left eye.

Fatina quivered. Abdullah always made sure to emphasize that Habiba was a "little Fatina." But no matter how much he said it, she was happy to hear it over and over. "Only her eyes are full of sparkle.... Abood, how long can we keep up this act with Habiba? What do parents here do? I try to think about when I started to realize all the harsh facts about the occupation, and I can't remember exactly when that was. Looking at how inquisitive she is, it breaks my heart to think of how she'll discover the reality of the world she lives in. I want her to be a normal child ... if that's even possible in Gaza."

Abdullah rubbed Fatina's shoulder as he relaxed his head against hers. In situations like this, he felt like he was trying to solve a puzzle. He believed in the nobility of his people's cause, but he also realized that it didn't come without struggle and sacrifice.

After Omar was killed, Abdullah felt as if a suffocating force was sucking the life out of him. All of Gaza seemed to be closing in on him. No matter where he went, it was all the same. Even the beach, which was the one place open to his people, was not open to Palestinians to travel through. Palestinians could enjoy the view and the water, but they couldn't travel by sea to any part of the outside world. But if he was willing to continue this battle, he had to equip his mind with more power than his body. He'd even started reading books about the power of the human brain.

Before Abdullah responded, he recalled a conversation that he and Fatina had had a while back: "Listen to this, Lulu. It says here that whatever you tell your brain, your subconscious mind will believe."

"Is that like playing tricks on one's own mind?" Fatina questioned.

"It makes sense. If you tell your mind something for a long period of time, you'll start to believe it. And if you visualize it, eventually, it will happen," Abdullah replied. "So that's why we should always think positive thoughts."

"But we have to really believe what we're telling our brains, don't we?" Fatina asked.

"Of course," Abdullah answered. "Believing it is the key."

Abdullah wanted to quell Fatina's fears, so he thought long and hard about that conversation before he replied to her. "As Habiba grows up, so will her mind. Her stamina and her ability to understand and accept things will also grow. And instead of accepting things, she may decide to challenge them.

We can't promise her the fairy-tale world that she reads about in her storybooks. But we can teach her that she can get what she wants if she sets her mind to it. We're not fooling her. We're helping her live this phase of her life to the best of her ability with the cards she was dealt. She'll be OK."

CLOSURE

As Fatina began to see the bigger picture of every-
thing we'd been through, it was as if she'd opened
the curtains and could finally see the world
outside her window. She was content and began
to get a grip on her life. It took years of pain and
anguish, but, in the end, she came out strong.
—Abdullah

Abdullah and Fatina survived the numerous Israeli
attacks. There was thrill and heartache in survival. But
bidding good-bye to the ones who had been killed was
heart-wrenching.

"You know Abood, I think I've figured it all out and
made my decision," Fatina said one day in the early fall
of 2014.

"Oh, yeah? What's that my brilliant wife?" Abdullah
was pleased with how much he and Fatina had grown

mentally and emotionally. It made him realize how invincible people could be if they wanted to.

"Those childhood stories were real after all," she replied. "You know, the battle between good and evil? There are good guys, and there are bad guys. That pretty much sums up our battle here on Earth. If we give up, we lose. The end."

Abdullah was happy to hear that his wife was finally coming around. For months, he'd been trying to convince her to visit a doctor, but she always protested. "Abood, I'm not in the right state of mind to bring another baby into this world. I keep thinking about the bombings and air strikes, and it paralyzes my thinking."

Fatina and Abdullah weren't as prolific in the baby department as the vast majority of Palestinian couples. Abdullah's mother kept nagging them to try to have another baby, but Fatina was uneasy when it came to talking about having children. She had been completely shell-shocked by the most recent attacks and was relieved that she didn't have any more kids whose safety and protection she couldn't guarantee.

But at the same time, another force was building up inside her. It was a battle of sheer existence. The Israelis wanted to suppress and kill her people. But Fatina realized that by surviving and thriving, the Palestinians could show the Israelis—and the world—that they were not going to stand for it. No one in her city had ever surrendered to the occupation, and Fatina was adamant to keep it that way.

To Abdullah, their whole life was precarious, but his belief in God and what He had in store for them gave him peace. "Habibti, you have to trust in Allah that good things will come our way. We aren't destined to live this kind of life forever," he said, hoping that his pep talk would raise Fatina's spirits. "Think happy thoughts. If you're putting your life on hold, it means you've surrendered, and I know you're not one to give up."

Fatina pressed her hands against her forehead. She tried to make sense of her husband's words. She trusted his judgment and knew that she had to keep moving forward. "Abood, will you be a fighter all of your life? Will my brothers be fighters all their lives? Is there no other way but to keep fighting?"

They were both sitting on the grass at a small park watching Habiba play. Abdullah said, "Whoa! There's been a major shift in your thinking! Remember when we first met how you thought that the Resistance was enchanting? But to soothe your soul, my love, I'll say this: We're not bloodthirsty people. There will come a day when we can just go back to our land without having to keep fighting. But for the time being, we're being forced to fight simply because we keep getting attacked."

Abdullah drew Fatina closer to him. "Hey, close your eyes and picture a big old house with two dunams of land full of orange and olive groves. There are children playing in the sand and climbing trees. They pick oranges and eat them right off the tree. Habiba has a brother named Omar. They play hide-and-seek. Habiba is a teenager and has her own interests, so Omar brings over his friends to play. He's a mischievous boy. Habiba is in love with our next-door neighbor's twenty-five-year-old son. He's a doctor and knows nothing about the old days when his father was in the Resistance. He's aristocratic—nothing like me."

Fatina looked up and giggled, "Does that mean he's arrogant? If he's someone who looks down upon people like us, I would never allow Habiba to marry him."

"No, he's not snobbish at all. He's handsome, peaceful, and romantic. His name is Ali. When he comes to ask for Habiba's hand in marriage, we both agree. But after a few months of marriage, he decides to fly off to Canada and see how life is in that part of the world. Just have these thoughts for now, Lulu, and you'll find peace."

Abdullah and Fatina sat watching Habiba kick a ball with all her strength. She clapped to herself, yelling, "Daddy, look!"

Abdullah opened up his arms as Habiba ran toward him. "You're getting stronger!" Abdullah stood up and tossed Habiba in the air. Her screams of delight reinvigorated his soul.

A few months later, around the time Habiba turned eight, Fatina and Abdullah conceived their second baby. Without any argument, they both agreed that he would be named Omar.

Fatina continued to snoop in Abdullah's diary from time to time. Sometimes, she would write replies to some of his entries:

I don't know how I can possibly express in words what I feel toward you. We've been together eleven years now, and my love for you hasn't diminished a bit. When I married you, I realized that our life together would not be a fairy tale. But the love you've given me has been unlike anything I ever seen in a romantic movie or soap opera. If I didn't know that you were a freedom fighter and was asked to give you a job title, the first thing that would come to mind when I look into your eyes would be a healer. You've helped me heal despite your sorrow. You've helped me reassemble the broken pieces of my life that left me distraught and hopeless. I can't say I gave as much back to you in return. Abood, you're a healer, you're a freedom fighter, and you're my hero.

—Fatina

THE END

Acknowledgements

This story would not have seen the light if it weren't for many wonderful people. Great minds and beautifully aesthetic people have imbued their magic in this story of Palestinian love and resilience. I'm grateful to any person who has assisted me in any way in the process of writing, editing and publishing. The support of my precious family has always been the rock which gave me fortitude and the power to go on. I want to thank my parents, my husband Samih, my children, my brother Mohanad, and my sisters Reham and Hoda.

Despite the many perilous circumstances Gaza has gone through in the process of publishing this book, I'm proud to say that my book has made it. It has emerged from the darkness of the jungle to reach my readers outside Gaza Strip.

It wasn't without pains and uncertainty that this book came to be. That's why I'm obliged to thank all those who believed in me and provided moral support encouraging me to be bold and accomplish my mission. In this regard, I'd like to thank a group of faithful friends— Ahmed Alnaouq, Tarneem Hammad, Ghada Ahmed, and Omnia Ghassan.

I'd like to send my heartfelt thanks to the meticulous and judicial editors, Katharine Sands and Jennifer Huston, who helped to bring out the moments of the book in a most refined manner. Thanks also go out to my book designer, David Provolo for his fascinating work.

I'm most thankful to my graceful producer, Domini Dragoone, who worked from the heart and soul employing her outstanding stylistic powers in every section of the book to bring out the story in the most captivating manner.

I'm indebted to Don Jacques and Kevin Hadduck whose eagle-eye editing, feedback, and advice guided and inspired me in multiple ways.

About the Author

Rana is a Palestinian writer from Gaza, Palestine. She specializes in English language training, testing and translation. Working with young people has given her a chance to understand their dreams and the energy that lies within. Rana sees her job as a chance to instill hope and motivation in the lives of the young people so they may take steps towards realizing their dreams. Her first book, *In Gaza, I Dare to Dream*, was published in 2016. Rana has published articles relating to life in Gaza under the 12 year-old blockade and the recurring assaults launched on Gaza Strip. She's also an activist and has published articles on the Great Return March on numerous sites. She is a mother of three and hopes one day her children will travel to see the world that exists outside Gaza.